Selected Works of
John Keats

ISBN: 978-1-62943-009-6

CONTENTS

Selected Works of John Keats

ON FIRST LOOKING INTO CHAPMAN'S HOMER

Much have I travell'd in the realms of gold,
And many goodly states and kingdoms seen;
Round many western islands have I been
Which bards in fealty to Apollo hold.
Oft of one wide expanse had I been told
That deep-brow'd Homer ruled as his demesne;
Yet did I never breathe its pure serene
Till I heard Chapman speak out loud and bold:
Then felt I like some watcher of the skies
When a new planet swims into his ken;
Or like stout Cortez when with eagle eyes
He star'd at the Pacific — and all his men
Look'd at each other with a wild surmise —
Silent, upon a peak in Darien.

ODE TO A NIGHTINGALE

I.

My heart aches, and a drowsy numbness pains
  My sense, as though of hemlock I had drunk,
Or emptied some dull opiate to the drains
  One minute past, and Lethe-wards had sunk:
'Tis not through envy of thy happy lot,
  But being too happy in thine happiness,—
    That thou, light-winged Dryad of the trees,
        In some melodious plot
  Of beechen green, and shadows numberless,
    Singest of summer in full-throated ease.

II.

O, for a draught of vintage! that hath been
  Cool'd a long age in the deep-delved earth,
Tasting of Flora and the country green,
  Dance, and Provencal song, and sunburnt mirth!
O for a beaker full of the warm South,
  Full of the true, the blushful Hippocrene,
    With beaded bubbles winking at the brim,

And purple-stained mouth;
  That I might drink, and leave the world unseen,
  And with thee fade away into the forest dim:

III.

Fade far away, dissolve, and quite forget
  What thou among the leaves hast never known,
The weariness, the fever, and the fret
  Here, where men sit and hear each other groan;
Where palsy shakes a few, sad, last gray hairs,
  Where youth grows pale, and spectre-thin, and dies;
    Where but to think is to be full of sorrow
      And leaden-eyed despairs,
  Where Beauty cannot keep her lustrous eyes,
    Or new Love pine at them beyond to-morrow.

IV.

Away! away! for I will fly to thee,
  Not charioted by Bacchus and his pards,
But on the viewless wings of Poesy,
  Though the dull brain perplexes and retards:
Already with thee! tender is the night,
  And haply the Queen-Moon is on her throne,
    Cluster'd around by all her starry Fays;
      But here there is no light,
  Save what from heaven is with the breezes blown
    Through verdurous glooms and winding mossy ways.

V.

I cannot see what flowers are at my feet,
  Nor what soft incense hangs upon the boughs,
But, in embalmed darkness, guess each sweet
  Wherewith the seasonable month endows
The grass, the thicket, and the fruit-tree wild;

White hawthorn, and the pastoral eglantine;
  Fast fading violets cover'd up in leaves;
    And mid-May's eldest child,
  The coming musk-rose, full of dewy wine,
    The murmurous haunt of flies on summer eves.

VI.

Darkling I listen; and, for many a time
  I have been half in love with easeful Death,
Call'd him soft names in many a mused rhyme,
  To take into the air my quiet breath;
Now more than ever seems it rich to die,
  To cease upon the midnight with no pain,
    While thou art pouring forth thy soul abroad
      In such an ecstasy!
  Still wouldst thou sing, and I have ears in vain—
    To thy high requiem become a sod.

VII.

Thou wast not born for death, immortal Bird!
  No hungry generations tread thee down;
The voice I hear this passing night was heard
  In ancient days by emperor and clown:
Perhaps the self-same song that found a path
  Through the sad heart of Ruth, when, sick for home,
    She stood in tears amid the alien corn;
      The same that oft-times hath
  Charm'd magic casements, opening on the foam
    Of perilous seas, in faery lands forlorn.

VIII.

Forlorn! the very word is like a bell
  To toll me back from thee to my sole self!
Adieu! the fancy cannot cheat so well

As she is fam'd to do, deceiving elf.
Adieu! adieu! thy plaintive anthem fades
   Past the near meadows, over the still stream,
      Up the hill-side; and now 'tis buried deep
            In the next valley-glades:
      Was it a vision, or a waking dream?
         Fled is that music:—Do I wake or sleep?

TO AUTUMN

Season of mists and mellow fruitfulness!
 Close bosom-friend of the maturing sun;
Conspiring with him how to load and bless
 With fruit the vines that round the thatch-eaves run;
To bend with apples the moss'd cottage-trees,
 And fill all fruit with ripeness to the core;
  To swell the gourd, and plump the hazel shells
 With a sweet kernel; to set budding more,
And still more, later flowers for the bees,
Until they think warm days will never cease,
 For Summer has o'er-brimm'd their clammy cells.

Who hath not seen thee oft amid thy store?
 Sometimes whoever seeks abroad may find
Thee sitting careless on a granary floor,
 Thy hair soft-lifted by the winnowing wind,
Or on a half-reap'd furrow sound asleep,
 Drowsed with the fume of poppies, while thy hook
  Spares the next swath and all its twinèd flowers;
And sometimes like a gleaner thou dost keep
 Steady thy laden head across a brook;
 Or by a cider-press, with patient look,

Thou watchest the last oozings hours by hours.

Where are the songs of Spring? Ay, where are they?
 Think not of them, thou hast thy music too,—
While barrèd clouds bloom the soft-dying day,
 And touch the stubble-plains with rosy hue;
Then in a wailful choir the small gnats mourn
 Among the river sallows, borne aloft
 Or sinking as the light wind lives or dies;
And full-grown lambs loud bleat from hilly bourn;
 Hedge-crickets sing; and now with treble soft
 The redbreast whistles from a garden-croft;
 And gathering swallows twitter in the skies.

BRIGHT STAR

Bright star, would I were stedfast as thou art—
Not in lone splendour hung aloft the night
And watching, with eternal lids apart,
Like nature's patient, sleepless Eremite,
The moving waters at their priestlike task
Of pure ablution round earth's human shores,
Or gazing on the new soft-fallen mask
Of snow upon the mountains and the moors
No—yet still stedfast, still unchangeable,
Pillow'd upon my fair love's ripening breast,
To feel for ever its soft fall and swell,
Awake for ever in a sweet unrest,
Still, still to hear her tender-taken breath,
And so live ever—or else swoon to death.

LA BELLE DAME SANS MERCI

O what can ail thee, knight at arms,
    Alone and palely loitering?
The sedge has wither'd from the lake,
    And no birds sing.

O What can ail thee, knight at arms,
    So haggard and so woe-begone?
The squirrel's granary is full,
    And the harvest's done.

I see a lily on thy brow
    With anguish moist and fever dew,
And on thy cheeks a fading rose
    Fast withereth too.

I met a lady in the meads,
    Full beautiful, a fairy's child;
Her hair was long, her foot was light,
    And her eyes were wild.

I made a garland for her head,
    And bracelets too, and fragrant zone;

She look'd at me as she did love,
  And made sweet moan.

I set her on my pacing steed,
  And nothing else saw all day long,
For sidelong would she bend, and sing
  A fairy's song.

She found me roots of relish sweet,
  And honey wild, and manna dew,
And sure in language strange she said—
  I love thee true.

She took me to her elfin grot,
  And there she wept, and sigh'd full sore,
And there I shut her wild wild eyes
  With kisses four.

And there she lulled me asleep,
  And there I dream'd—Ah! woe betide!
The latest dream I ever dream'd
  On the cold hill's side.

I saw pale kings, and princes too,
  Pale warriors, death pale were they all;
They cried—"La belle dame sans merci
  Hath thee in thrall!"

I saw their starv'd lips in the gloam
  With horrid warning gaped wide,
And I awoke and found me here
  On the cold hill's side.

And this is why I sojourn here,
  Alone and palely loitering,
Though the sedge is wither'd from the lake,
  And no birds sing.

LAMIA

Part I

Upon a time, before the faery broods
Drove Nymph and Satyr from the prosperous woods,
Before King Oberon's bright diadem,
Sceptre, and mantle, clasp'd with dewy gem,
Frighted away the Dryads and the Fauns
From rushes green, and brakes, and cowslip'd lawns,
The ever-smitten Hermes empty left
His golden throne, bent warm on amorous theft:
From high Olympus had he stolen light,
On this side of Jove's clouds, to escape the sight
Of his great summoner, and made retreat
Into a forest on the shores of Crete.
For somewhere in that sacred island dwelt
A nymph, to whom all hoofed Satyrs knelt;
At whose white feet the languid Tritons poured
Pearls, while on land they wither'd and adored.
Fast by the springs where she to bathe was wont,
And in those meads where sometime she might haunt,
Were strewn rich gifts, unknown to any Muse,
Though Fancy's casket were unlock'd to choose.
Ah, what a world of love was at her feet!

So Hermes thought, and a celestial heat
Burnt from his winged heels to either ear,
That from a whiteness, as the lily clear,
Blush'd into roses 'mid his golden hair,
Fallen in jealous curls about his shoulders bare.
From vale to vale, from wood to wood, he flew,
Breathing upon the flowers his passion new,
And wound with many a river to its head,
To find where this sweet nymph prepar'd her secret bed:
In vain; the sweet nymph might nowhere be found,
And so he rested, on the lonely ground,
Pensive, and full of painful jealousies
Of the Wood-Gods, and even the very trees.
There as he stood, he heard a mournful voice,
Such as once heard, in gentle heart, destroys
All pain but pity: thus the lone voice spake:
"When from this wreathed tomb shall I awake!
"When move in a sweet body fit for life,
"And love, and pleasure, and the ruddy strife
"Of hearts and lips! Ah, miserable me!"
The God, dove-footed, glided silently
Round bush and tree, soft-brushing, in his speed,
The taller grasses and full-flowering weed,
Until he found a palpitating snake,
Bright, and cirque-couchant in a dusky brake.

   She was a gordian shape of dazzling hue,
Vermilion-spotted, golden, green, and blue;
Striped like a zebra, freckled like a pard,
Eyed like a peacock, and all crimson barr'd;
And full of silver moons, that, as she breathed,
Dissolv'd, or brighter shone, or interwreathed
Their lustres with the gloomier tapestries—
So rainbow-sided, touch'd with miseries,
She seem'd, at once, some penanced lady elf,
Some demon's mistress, or the demon's self.
Upon her crest she wore a wannish fire
Sprinkled with stars, like Ariadne's tiar:

Her head was serpent, but ah, bitter-sweet!
She had a woman's mouth with all its pearls complete:
And for her eyes: what could such eyes do there
But weep, and weep, that they were born so fair?
As Proserpine still weeps for her Sicilian air.
Her throat was serpent, but the words she spake
Came, as through bubbling honey, for Love's sake,
And thus; while Hermes on his pinions lay,
Like a stoop'd falcon ere he takes his prey.

    "Fair Hermes, crown'd with feathers, fluttering light,
"I had a splendid dream of thee last night:
"I saw thee sitting, on a throne of gold,
"Among the Gods, upon Olympus old,
"The only sad one; for thou didst not hear
"The soft, lute-finger'd Muses chaunting clear,
"Nor even Apollo when he sang alone,
"Deaf to his throbbing throat's long, long melodious moan.
"I dreamt I saw thee, robed in purple flakes,
"Break amorous through the clouds, as morning breaks,
"And, swiftly as a bright Phoebean dart,
"Strike for the Cretan isle; and here thou art!
"Too gentle Hermes, hast thou found the maid?"
Whereat the star of Lethe not delay'd
His rosy eloquence, and thus inquired:
"Thou smooth-lipp'd serpent, surely high inspired!
"Thou beauteous wreath, with melancholy eyes,
"Possess whatever bliss thou canst devise,
"Telling me only where my nymph is fled,——
"Where she doth breathe!" "Bright planet, thou hast said,"
Return'd the snake, "but seal with oaths, fair God!"
"I swear," said Hermes, "by my serpent rod,
"And by thine eyes, and by thy starry crown!"
Light flew his earnest words, among the blossoms blown.
Then thus again the brilliance feminine:
"Too frail of heart! for this lost nymph of thine,
"Free as the air, invisibly, she strays
"About these thornless wilds; her pleasant days

"She tastes unseen; unseen her nimble feet
"Leave traces in the grass and flowers sweet;
"From weary tendrils, and bow'd branches green,
"She plucks the fruit unseen, she bathes unseen:
"And by my power is her beauty veil'd
"To keep it unaffronted, unassail'd
"By the love-glances of unlovely eyes,
"Of Satyrs, Fauns, and blear'd Silenus' sighs.
"Pale grew her immortality, for woe
"Of all these lovers, and she grieved so
"I took compassion on her, bade her steep
"Her hair in weird syrops, that would keep
"Her loveliness invisible, yet free
"To wander as she loves, in liberty.
"Thou shalt behold her, Hermes, thou alone,
"If thou wilt, as thou swearest, grant my boon!"
Then, once again, the charmed God began
An oath, and through the serpent's ears it ran
Warm, tremulous, devout, psalterian.
Ravish'd, she lifted her Circean head,
Blush'd a live damask, and swift-lisping said,
"I was a woman, let me have once more
"A woman's shape, and charming as before.
"I love a youth of Corinth—O the bliss!
"Give me my woman's form, and place me where he is.
"Stoop, Hermes, let me breathe upon thy brow,
"And thou shalt see thy sweet nymph even now."
The God on half-shut feathers sank serene,
She breath'd upon his eyes, and swift was seen
Of both the guarded nymph near-smiling on the green.
It was no dream; or say a dream it was,
Real are the dreams of Gods, and smoothly pass
Their pleasures in a long immortal dream.
One warm, flush'd moment, hovering, it might seem
Dash'd by the wood-nymph's beauty, so he burn'd;
Then, lighting on the printless verdure, turn'd
To the swoon'd serpent, and with languid arm,

Delicate, put to proof the lythe Caducean charm.
So done, upon the nymph his eyes he bent,
Full of adoring tears and blandishment,
And towards her stept: she, like a moon in wane,
Faded before him, cower'd, nor could restrain
Her fearful sobs, self-folding like a flower
That faints into itself at evening hour:
But the God fostering her chilled hand,
She felt the warmth, her eyelids open'd bland,
And, like new flowers at morning song of bees,
Bloom'd, and gave up her honey to the lees.
Into the green-recessed woods they flew;
Nor grew they pale, as mortal lovers do.
    Left to herself, the serpent now began
To change; her elfin blood in madness ran,
Her mouth foam'd, and the grass, therewith besprent,
Wither'd at dew so sweet and virulent;
Her eyes in torture fix'd, and anguish drear,
Hot, glaz'd, and wide, with lid-lashes all sear,
Flash'd phosphor and sharp sparks, without one cooling
tear.
The colours all inflam'd throughout her train,
She writh'd about, convuls'd with scarlet pain:
A deep volcanian yellow took the place
Of all her milder-mooned body's grace;
And, as the lava ravishes the mead,
Spoilt all her silver mail, and golden brede;
Made gloom of all her frecklings, streaks and bars,
Eclips'd her crescents, and lick'd up her stars:
So that, in moments few, she was undrest
Of all her sapphires, greens, and amethyst,
And rubious-argent: of all these bereft,
Nothing but pain and ugliness were left.
Still shone her crown; that vanish'd, also she
Melted and disappear'd as suddenly;
And in the air, her new voice luting soft,
Cried, "Lycius! gentle Lycius!"——Borne aloft

With the bright mists about the mountains hoar
These words dissolv'd: Crete's forests heard no more.
　　Whither fled Lamia, now a lady bright,
A full-born beauty new and exquisite?
She fled into that valley they pass o'er
Who go to Corinth from Cenchreas' shore;
And rested at the foot of those wild hills,
The rugged founts of the Peraean rills,
And of that other ridge whose barren back
Stretches, with all its mist and cloudy rack,
South-westward to Cleone. There she stood
About a young bird's flutter from a wood,
Fair, on a sloping green of mossy tread,
By a clear pool, wherein she passioned
To see herself escap'd from so sore ills,
While her robes flaunted with the daffodils.
　　Ah, happy Lycius!——for she was a maid
More beautiful than ever twisted braid,
Or sigh'd, or blush'd, or on spring-flowered lea
Spread a green kirtle to the minstrelsy:
A virgin purest lipp'd, yet in the lore
Of love deep learned to the red heart's core:
Not one hour old, yet of sciential brain
To unperplex bliss from its neighbour pain;
Define their pettish limits, and estrange
Their points of contact, and swift counterchange;
Intrigue with the specious chaos, and dispart
Its most ambiguous atoms with sure art;
As though in Cupid's college she had spent
Sweet days a lovely graduate, still unshent,
And kept his rosy terms in idle languishment.
　　Why this fair creature chose so fairily
By the wayside to linger, we shall see;
But first 'tis fit to tell how she could muse
And dream, when in the serpent prison-house,
Of all she list, strange or magnificent:
How, ever, where she will'd, her spirit went;

Whether to faint Elysium, or where
Down through tress-lifting waves the Nereids fair
Wind into Thetis' bower by many a pearly stair;
Or where God Bacchus drains his cups divine,
Stretch'd out, at ease, beneath a glutinous pine;
Or where in Pluto's gardens palatine
Mulciber's columns gleam in far piazzian line.
And sometimes into cities she would send
Her dream, with feast and rioting to blend;
And once, while among mortals dreaming thus,
She saw the young Corinthian Lycius
Charioting foremost in the envious race,
Like a young Jove with calm uneager face,
And fell into a swooning love of him.
Now on the moth-time of that evening dim
He would return that way, as well she knew,
To Corinth from the shore; for freshly blew
The eastern soft wind, and his galley now
Grated the quaystones with her brazen prow
In port Cenchreas, from Egina isle
Fresh anchor'd; whither he had been awhile
To sacrifice to Jove, whose temple there
Waits with high marble doors for blood and incense rare.
Jove heard his vows, and better'd his desire;
For by some freakful chance he made retire
From his companions, and set forth to walk,
Perhaps grown wearied of their Corinth talk:
Over the solitary hills he fared,
Thoughtless at first, but ere eve's star appeared
His phantasy was lost, where reason fades,
In the calm'd twilight of Platonic shades.
Lamia beheld him coming, near, more near—
Close to her passing, in indifference drear,
His silent sandals swept the mossy green;
So neighbour'd to him, and yet so unseen
She stood: he pass'd, shut up in mysteries,
His mind wrapp'd like his mantle, while her eyes

Follow'd his steps, and her neck regal white
Turn'd——syllabling thus, "Ah, Lycius bright,
"And will you leave me on the hills alone?
"Lycius, look back! and be some pity shown."
He did; not with cold wonder fearingly,
But Orpheus-like at an Eurydice;
For so delicious were the words she sung,
It seem'd he had lov'd them a whole summer long:
And soon his eyes had drunk her beauty up,
Leaving no drop in the bewildering cup,
And still the cup was full,——while he afraid
Lest she should vanish ere his lip had paid
Due adoration, thus began to adore;
Her soft look growing coy, she saw his chain so sure:
"Leave thee alone! Look back! Ah, Goddess, see
"Whether my eyes can ever turn from thee!
"For pity do not this sad heart belie——
"Even as thou vanishest so I shall die.
"Stay! though a Naiad of the rivers, stay!
"To thy far wishes will thy streams obey:
"Stay! though the greenest woods be thy domain,
"Alone they can drink up the morning rain:
"Though a descended Pleiad, will not one
"Of thine harmonious sisters keep in tune
"Thy spheres, and as thy silver proxy shine?
"So sweetly to these ravish'd ears of mine
"Came thy sweet greeting, that if thou shouldst fade
"Thy memory will waste me to a shade:——
"For pity do not melt!"——"If I should stay,"
Said Lamia, "here, upon this floor of clay,
"And pain my steps upon these flowers too rough,
"What canst thou say or do of charm enough
"To dull the nice remembrance of my home?
"Thou canst not ask me with thee here to roam
"Over these hills and vales, where no joy is,——
"Empty of immortality and bliss!
"Thou art a scholar, Lycius, and must know

"That finer spirits cannot breathe below
"In human climes, and live: Alas! poor youth,
"What taste of purer air hast thou to soothe
"My essence? What serener palaces,
"Where I may all my many senses please,
"And by mysterious sleights a hundred thirsts appease?
"It cannot be——Adieu!" So said, she rose
Tiptoe with white arms spread. He, sick to lose
The amorous promise of her lone complain,
Swoon'd, murmuring of love, and pale with pain.
The cruel lady, without any show
Of sorrow for her tender favourite's woe,
But rather, if her eyes could brighter be,
With brighter eyes and slow amenity,
Put her new lips to his, and gave afresh
The life she had so tangled in her mesh:
And as he from one trance was wakening
Into another, she began to sing,
Happy in beauty, life, and love, and every thing,
A song of love, too sweet for earthly lyres,
While, like held breath, the stars drew in their panting fires
And then she whisper'd in such trembling tone,
As those who, safe together met alone
For the first time through many anguish'd days,
Use other speech than looks; bidding him raise
His drooping head, and clear his soul of doubt,
For that she was a woman, and without
Any more subtle fluid in her veins
Than throbbing blood, and that the self-same pains
Inhabited her frail-strung heart as his.
And next she wonder'd how his eyes could miss
Her face so long in Corinth, where, she said,
She dwelt but half retir'd, and there had led
Days happy as the gold coin could invent
Without the aid of love; yet in content
Till she saw him, as once she pass'd him by,
Where 'gainst a column he leant thoughtfully

At Venus' temple porch, 'mid baskets heap'd
Of amorous herbs and flowers, newly reap'd
Late on that eve, as 'twas the night before
The Adonian feast; whereof she saw no more,
But wept alone those days, for why should she adore?
Lycius from death awoke into amaze,
To see her still, and singing so sweet lays;
Then from amaze into delight he fell
To hear her whisper woman's lore so well;
And every word she spake entic'd him on
To unperplex'd delight and pleasure known.
Let the mad poets say whate'er they please
Of the sweets of Fairies, Peris, Goddesses,
There is not such a treat among them all,
Haunters of cavern, lake, and waterfall,
As a real woman, lineal indeed
From Pyrrha's pebbles or old Adam's seed.
Thus gentle Lamia judg'd, and judg'd aright,
That Lycius could not love in half a fright,
So threw the goddess off, and won his heart
More pleasantly by playing woman's part,
With no more awe than what her beauty gave,
That, while it smote, still guaranteed to save.
Lycius to all made eloquent reply,
Marrying to every word a twinborn sigh;
And last, pointing to Corinth, ask'd her sweet,
If 'twas too far that night for her soft feet.
The way was short, for Lamia's eagerness
Made, by a spell, the triple league decrease
To a few paces; not at all surmised
By blinded Lycius, so in her comprized.
They pass'd the city gates, he knew not how
So noiseless, and he never thought to know.

    As men talk in a dream, so Corinth all,
Throughout her palaces imperial,
And all her populous streets and temples lewd,
Mutter'd, like tempest in the distance brew'd,

To the wide-spreaded night above her towers.
Men, women, rich and poor, in the cool hours,
Shuffled their sandals o'er the pavement white,
Companion'd or alone; while many a light
Flared, here and there, from wealthy festivals,
And threw their moving shadows on the walls,
Or found them cluster'd in the corniced shade
Of some arch'd temple door, or dusky colonnade.
　　Muffling his face, of greeting friends in fear,
Her fingers he press'd hard, as one came near
With curl'd gray beard, sharp eyes, and smooth bald crown,
Slow-stepp'd, and robed in philosophic gown:
Lycius shrank closer, as they met and past,
Into his mantle, adding wings to haste,
While hurried Lamia trembled: "Ah," said he,
"Why do you shudder, love, so ruefully?
"Why does your tender palm dissolve in dew?"——
"I'm wearied," said fair Lamia: "tell me who
"Is that old man? I cannot bring to mind
"His features:——Lycius! wherefore did you blind
"Yourself from his quick eyes?" Lycius replied,
"'Tis Apollonius sage, my trusty guide
"And good instructor; but to-night he seems
"The ghost of folly haunting my sweet dreams.
　　While yet he spake they had arrived before
A pillar'd porch, with lofty portal door,
Where hung a silver lamp, whose phosphor glow
Reflected in the slabbed steps below,
Mild as a star in water; for so new,
And so unsullied was the marble hue,
So through the crystal polish, liquid fine,
Ran the dark veins, that none but feet divine
Could e'er have touch'd there. Sounds Aeolian
Breath'd from the hinges, as the ample span
Of the wide doors disclos'd a place unknown
Some time to any, but those two alone,
And a few Persian mutes, who that same year

Were seen about the markets: none knew where
They could inhabit; the most curious
Were foil'd, who watch'd to trace them to their house:
And but the flitter-winged verse must tell,
For truth's sake, what woe afterwards befel,
'Twould humour many a heart to leave them thus,
Shut from the busy world of more incredulous.

Part II

Love in a hut, with water and a crust,
Is—Love, forgive us!—cinders, ashes, dust;
Love in a palace is perhaps at last
More grievous torment than a hermit's fast:——
That is a doubtful tale from faery land,
Hard for the non-elect to understand.
Had Lycius liv'd to hand his story down,
He might have given the moral a fresh frown,
Or clench'd it quite: but too short was their bliss
To breed distrust and hate, that make the soft voice hiss.
Besides, there, nightly, with terrific glare,
Love, jealous grown of so complete a pair,
Hover'd and buzz'd his wings, with fearful roar,
Above the lintel of their chamber door,
And down the passage cast a glow upon the floor.
    For all this came a ruin: side by side
They were enthroned, in the even tide,
Upon a couch, near to a curtaining
Whose airy texture, from a golden string,
Floated into the room, and let appear
Unveil'd the summer heaven, blue and clear,
Betwixt two marble shafts:——there they reposed,
Where use had made it sweet, with eyelids closed,
Saving a tythe which love still open kept,
That they might see each other while they almost slept;
When from the slope side of a suburb hill,

22

Deafening the swallow's twitter, came a thrill
Of trumpets——Lycius started——the sounds fled,
But left a thought, a buzzing in his head.
For the first time, since first he harbour'd in
That purple-lined palace of sweet sin,
His spirit pass'd beyond its golden bourn
Into the noisy world almost forsworn.
The lady, ever watchful, penetrant,
Saw this with pain, so arguing a want
Of something more, more than her empery
Of joys; and she began to moan and sigh
Because he mused beyond her, knowing well
That but a moment's thought is passion's passing bell.
"Why do you sigh, fair creature?" whisper'd he:
"Why do you think?" return'd she tenderly:
"You have deserted me;——where am I now?
"Not in your heart while care weighs on your brow:
"No, no, you have dismiss'd me; and I go
"From your breast houseless: ay, it must be so."
He answer'd, bending to her open eyes,
Where he was mirror'd small in paradise,
"My silver planet, both of eve and morn!
"Why will you plead yourself so sad forlorn,
"While I am striving how to fill my heart
"With deeper crimson, and a double smart?
"How to entangle, trammel up and snare
"Your soul in mine, and labyrinth you there
"Like the hid scent in an unbudded rose?
"Ay, a sweet kiss——you see your mighty woes.
"My thoughts! shall I unveil them? Listen then!
"What mortal hath a prize, that other men
"May be confounded and abash'd withal,
"But lets it sometimes pace abroad majestical,
"And triumph, as in thee I should rejoice
"Amid the hoarse alarm of Corinth's voice.
"Let my foes choke, and my friends shout afar,
"While through the thronged streets your bridal car

"Wheels round its dazzling spokes."——The lady's cheek
Trembled; she nothing said, but, pale and meek,
Arose and knelt before him, wept a rain
Of sorrows at his words; at last with pain
Beseeching him, the while his hand she wrung,
To change his purpose. He thereat was stung,
Perverse, with stronger fancy to reclaim
Her wild and timid nature to his aim:
Besides, for all his love, in self despite,
Against his better self, he took delight
Luxurious in her sorrows, soft and new.
His passion, cruel grown, took on a hue
Fierce and sanguineous as 'twas possible
In one whose brow had no dark veins to swell.
Fine was the mitigated fury, like
Apollo's presence when in act to strike
The serpent——Ha, the serpent! certes, she
Was none. She burnt, she lov'd the tyranny,
And, all subdued, consented to the hour
When to the bridal he should lead his paramour.
Whispering in midnight silence, said the youth,
"Sure some sweet name thou hast, though, by my truth,
"I have not ask'd it, ever thinking thee
"Not mortal, but of heavenly progeny,
"As still I do. Hast any mortal name,
"Fit appellation for this dazzling frame?
"Or friends or kinsfolk on the citied earth,
"To share our marriage feast and nuptial mirth?"
"I have no friends," said Lamia, "no, not one;
"My presence in wide Corinth hardly known:
"My parents' bones are in their dusty urns
"Sepulchred, where no kindled incense burns,
"Seeing all their luckless race are dead, save me,
"And I neglect the holy rite for thee.
"Even as you list invite your many guests;
"But if, as now it seems, your vision rests
"With any pleasure on me, do not bid

"Old Apollonius—from him keep me hid."
Lycius, perplex'd at words so blind and blank,
Made close inquiry; from whose touch she shrank,
Feigning a sleep; and he to the dull shade
Of deep sleep in a moment was betray'd.
    It was the custom then to bring away
The bride from home at blushing shut of day,
Veil'd, in a chariot, heralded along
By strewn flowers, torches, and a marriage song,
With other pageants: but this fair unknown
Had not a friend. So being left alone,
(Lycius was gone to summon all his kin)
And knowing surely she could never win
His foolish heart from its mad pompousness,
She set herself, high-thoughted, how to dress
The misery in fit magnificence.
She did so, but 'tis doubtful how and whence
Came, and who were her subtle servitors.
About the halls, and to and from the doors,
There was a noise of wings, till in short space
The glowing banquet-room shone with wide-arched grace.
A haunting music, sole perhaps and lone
Supportress of the faery-roof, made moan
Throughout, as fearful the whole charm might fade.
Fresh carved cedar, mimicking a glade
Of palm and plantain, met from either side,
High in the midst, in honour of the bride:
Two palms and then two plantains, and so on,
From either side their stems branch'd one to one
All down the aisled place; and beneath all
There ran a stream of lamps straight on from wall to wall.
So canopied, lay an untasted feast
Teeming with odours. Lamia, regal drest,
Silently paced about, and as she went,
In pale contented sort of discontent,
Mission'd her viewless servants to enrich
The fretted splendour of each nook and niche.

Between the tree-stems, marbled plain at first,
Came jasper pannels; then, anon, there burst
Forth creeping imagery of slighter trees,
And with the larger wove in small intricacies.
Approving all, she faded at self-will,
And shut the chamber up, close, hush'd and still,
Complete and ready for the revels rude,
When dreadful guests would come to spoil her solitude.
    The day appear'd, and all the gossip rout.
O senseless Lycius! Madman! wherefore flout
The silent-blessing fate, warm cloister'd hours,
And show to common eyes these secret bowers?
The herd approach'd; each guest, with busy brain,
Arriving at the portal, gaz'd amain,
And enter'd marveling: for they knew the street,
Remember'd it from childhood all complete
Without a gap, yet ne'er before had seen
That royal porch, that high-built fair demesne;
So in they hurried all, maz'd, curious and keen:
Save one, who look'd thereon with eye severe,
And with calm-planted steps walk'd in austere;
'Twas Apollonius: something too he laugh'd,
As though some knotty problem, that had daft
His patient thought, had now begun to thaw,
And solve and melt:——'twas just as he foresaw.
    He met within the murmurous vestibule
His young disciple. "'Tis no common rule,
"Lycius," said he, "for uninvited guest
"To force himself upon you, and infest
"With an unbidden presence the bright throng
"Of younger friends; yet must I do this wrong,
"And you forgive me." Lycius blush'd, and led
The old man through the inner doors broad-spread;
With reconciling words and courteous mien
Turning into sweet milk the sophist's spleen.
    Of wealthy lustre was the banquet-room,
Fill'd with pervading brilliance and perfume:

Before each lucid pannel fuming stood
A censer fed with myrrh and spiced wood,
Each by a sacred tripod held aloft,
Whose slender feet wide-swerv'd upon the soft
Wool-woofed carpets: fifty wreaths of smoke
From fifty censers their light voyage took
To the high roof, still mimick'd as they rose
Along the mirror'd walls by twin-clouds odorous.
Twelve sphered tables, by silk seats insphered,
High as the level of a man's breast rear'd
On libbard's paws, upheld the heavy gold
Of cups and goblets, and the store thrice told
Of Ceres' horn, and, in huge vessels, wine
Came from the gloomy tun with merry shine.
Thus loaded with a feast the tables stood,
Each shrining in the midst the image of a God.
   When in an antichamber every guest
Had felt the cold full sponge to pleasure press'd,
By minist'ring slaves, upon his hands and feet,
And fragrant oils with ceremony meet
Pour'd on his hair, they all mov'd to the feast
In white robes, and themselves in order placed
Around the silken couches, wondering
Whence all this mighty cost and blaze of wealth could
spring.
   Soft went the music the soft air along,
While fluent Greek a vowel'd undersong
Kept up among the guests discoursing low
At first, for scarcely was the wine at flow;
But when the happy vintage touch'd their brains,
Louder they talk, and louder come the strains
Of powerful instruments:——the gorgeous dyes,
The space, the splendour of the draperies,
The roof of awful richness, nectarous cheer,
Beautiful slaves, and Lamia's self, appear,
Now, when the wine has done its rosy deed,
And every soul from human trammels freed,

No more so strange; for merry wine, sweet wine,
Will make Elysian shades not too fair, too divine.
Soon was God Bacchus at meridian height;
Flush'd were their cheeks, and bright eyes double bright:
Garlands of every green, and every scent
From vales deflower'd, or forest-trees branch rent,
In baskets of bright osier'd gold were brought
High as the handles heap'd, to suit the thought
Of every guest; that each, as he did please,
Might fancy-fit his brows, silk-pillow'd at his ease.

    What wreath for Lamia? What for Lycius?
What for the sage, old Apollonius?
Upon her aching forehead be there hung
The leaves of willow and of adder's tongue;
And for the youth, quick, let us strip for him
The thyrsus, that his watching eyes may swim
Into forgetfulness; and, for the sage,
Let spear-grass and the spiteful thistle wage
War on his temples. Do not all charms fly
At the mere touch of cold philosophy?
There was an awful rainbow once in heaven:
We know her woof, her texture; she is given
In the dull catalogue of common things.
Philosophy will clip an Angel's wings,
Conquer all mysteries by rule and line,
Empty the haunted air, and gnomed mine——
Unweave a rainbow, as it erewhile made
The tender-person'd Lamia melt into a shade.

    By her glad Lycius sitting, in chief place,
Scarce saw in all the room another face,
Till, checking his love trance, a cup he took
Full brimm'd, and opposite sent forth a look
'Cross the broad table, to beseech a glance
From his old teacher's wrinkled countenance,
And pledge him. The bald-head philosopher
Had fix'd his eye, without a twinkle or stir
Full on the alarmed beauty of the bride,

Brow-beating her fair form, and troubling her sweet pride.
Lycius then press'd her hand, with devout touch,
As pale it lay upon the rosy couch:
'Twas icy, and the cold ran through his veins;
Then sudden it grew hot, and all the pains
Of an unnatural heat shot to his heart.
"Lamia, what means this? Wherefore dost thou start?
"Know'st thou that man?" Poor Lamia answer'd not.
He gaz'd into her eyes, and not a jot
Own'd they the lovelorn piteous appeal:
More, more he gaz'd: his human senses reel:
Some hungry spell that loveliness absorbs;
There was no recognition in those orbs.
"Lamia!" he cried——and no soft-toned reply.
The many heard, and the loud revelry
Grew hush; the stately music no more breathes;
The myrtle sicken'd in a thousand wreaths.
By faint degrees, voice, lute, and pleasure ceased;
A deadly silence step by step increased,
Until it seem'd a horrid presence there,
And not a man but felt the terror in his hair.
"Lamia!" he shriek'd; and nothing but the shriek
With its sad echo did the silence break.
"Begone, foul dream!" he cried, gazing again
In the bride's face, where now no azure vein
Wander'd on fair-spaced temples; no soft bloom
Misted the cheek; no passion to illume
The deep-recessed vision:——all was blight;
Lamia, no longer fair, there sat a deadly white.
"Shut, shut those juggling eyes, thou ruthless man!
"Turn them aside, wretch! or the righteous ban
"Of all the Gods, whose dreadful images
"Here represent their shadowy presences,
"May pierce them on the sudden with the thorn
"Of painful blindness; leaving thee forlorn,
"In trembling dotage to the feeblest fright
"Of conscience, for their long offended might,

"For all thine impious proud-heart sophistries,
"Unlawful magic, and enticing lies.
"Corinthians! look upon that gray-beard wretch!
"Mark how, possess'd, his lashless eyelids stretch
"Around his demon eyes! Corinthians, see!
"My sweet bride withers at their potency."
"Fool!" said the sophist, in an under-tone
Gruff with contempt; which a death-nighing moan
From Lycius answer'd, as heart-struck and lost,
He sank supine beside the aching ghost.
"Fool! Fool!" repeated he, while his eyes still
Relented not, nor mov'd; "from every ill
"Of life have I preserv'd thee to this day,
"And shall I see thee made a serpent's prey?
Then Lamia breath'd death breath; the sophist's eye,
Like a sharp spear, went through her utterly,
Keen, cruel, perceant, stinging: she, as well
As her weak hand could any meaning tell,
Motion'd him to be silent; vainly so,
He look'd and look'd again a level——No!
"A Serpent!" echoed he; no sooner said,
Than with a frightful scream she vanished:
And Lycius' arms were empty of delight,
As were his limbs of life, from that same night.
On the high couch he lay!——his friends came round——
Supported him——no pulse, or breath they found,
And, in its marriage robe, the heavy body wound.

ODE ON A GRECIAN URN

Thou still unravish'd bride of quietness!
 Thou foster-child of Silence and slow Time,
Sylvan historian, who canst thus express
 A flowery tale more sweetly than our rhyme:
What leaf-fringed legend haunts about thy shape
 Of deities or mortals, or of both,
  In Tempe or the dales of Arcady?
 What men or gods are these? what maidens loath?
What mad pursuit? What struggle to escape?
 What pipes and timbrels? What wild ecstasy?

Heard melodies are sweet, but those unheard
 Are sweeter; therefore, ye soft pipes, play on;
Not to the sensual ear, but, more endear'd,
 Pipe to the spirit ditties of no tone:
Fair youth, beneath the trees, thou canst not leave
 Thy song, nor ever can those trees be bare;
  Bold Lover, never, never canst thou kiss,
Though winning near the goal—yet, do not grieve;
 She cannot fade, though thou hast not thy bliss,
 Forever wilt thou love, and she be fair!

Ah, happy, happy boughs! that cannot shed
 Your leaves, nor ever bid the Spring adieu;
And, happy melodist, unwearied,
 Forever piping songs forever new;
More happy love! more happy, happy love!
 Forever warm and still to be enjoy'd,
 Forever panting and forever young;
All breathing human passion far above,
 That leaves a heart high sorrowful and cloy'd,
 A burning forehead and a parching tongue.

Who are these coming to the sacrifice?
 To what green altar, O mysterious priest,
Lead'st thou that heifer lowing at the skies,
 And all her silken flanks with garlands drest?
What little town by river or sea-shore,
 Or mountain-built with peaceful citadel,
 Is emptied of its folk, this pious morn?
And, little town, thy streets for evermore
 Will silent be; and not a soul to tell
 Why thou art desolate, can e'er return.

O Attic shape! Fair attitude! with brede
 Of marble men and maidens overwrought,
With forest branches and the trodden weed;
 Thou, silent form! dost tease us out of thought
As doth eternity: Cold Pastoral!
 When old age shall this generation waste,
 Thou shalt remain, in midst of other woe
 Than ours, a friend to man, to whom thou say'st,
"Beauty is truth, truth beauty,"—that is all
 Ye know on earth, and all ye need to know.

ODE ON INDOLENCE

They toil not, neither do they spin.

I

One morn before me were three figures seen,
With bowed necks, and joined hands, side-faced;
And one behind the other stepp'd serene,
In placid sandals, and in white robes graced;
They pass'd, like figures on a marble urn
When shifted round to see the other side;
They came again, as, when the urn once more
Is shifted round, the first seen shades return;
And they were strange to me, as may betide
With vases, to one deep in Phidian lore.

II

How is it, Shadows! that I knew ye not?
How came ye muffled in so hush a masque?
Was it a silent deep-disguised plot
To steal away, and leave without a task
My idle days? Ripe was the drowsy hour;
The blissful cloud of summer-indolence
Benumb'd my eyes; my pulse grew less and less;
Pain had no sting, and pleasure's wreath no flower:
O, why did ye not melt, and leave my sense

Unhaunted quite of all but-nothingness?

III

A third time came they by;- alas! wherefore?
My sleep had been embroider'd with dim dreams;
My soul had been a lawn besprinkled o'er
With flowers, and stirring shades, and baffled beams:
The morn was clouded, but no shower fell,
Though in her lids hung the sweet tears of May;
The open casement press'd a new-leav'd vine,
Let in the budding warmth and throstle's lay;
O Shadows! 'twas a time to bid farewell!
Upon your skirts had fallen no tears of mine.

IV

A third time pass'd they by, and, passing, turn'd
Each one the face a moment whiles to me;
Then faded, and to follow them I burn'd
And ach'd for wings because I knew the three;
The first was a fair Maid, and Love her name;
The second was Ambition, pale of cheek,
And ever watchful with fatigued eye;
The last, whom I love more, the more of blame
Is heap'd upon her, maiden most unmeek,-
I knew to be my demon Poesy.

V

They faded, and, forsooth! I wanted wings:
O folly! What is love! and where is it?
And for that poor Ambition! it springs
From a man's little heart's short fever-fit;
For Poesy!- no,- she has not a joy,-
At least for me,- so sweet as drowsy noons,
And evenings steep'd in honied indolence;
O, for an age so shelter'd from annoy,
That I may never know how change the moons,
Or hear the voice of busy common-sense!

VI

So, ye three Ghosts, adieu! Ye cannot raise
My head cool-bedded in the flowery grass;

For I would not be dieted with praise,
A pet-lamb in a sentimental farce!
Fade softly from my eyes, and be once more
In masque-like figures on the dreamy urn;
Farewell! I yet have visions for the night,
And for the day faint visions there is store;
Vanish, ye Phantoms! from my idle spright,
Into the clouds, and never more return!

ODE ON MELANCHOLY

No, no! go not to Lethe, neither twist
  Wolf's-bane, tight-rooted, for its poisonous wine;
Nor suffer thy pale forehead to be kiss'd
  By nightshade, ruby grape of Proserpine;
Make not your rosary of yew-berries,
  Nor let the beetle, nor the death-moth be
    Your mournful Psyche, nor the downy owl
A partner in your sorrow's mysteries;
  For shade to shade will come too drowsily,
    And drown the wakeful anguish of the soul.

But when the melancholy fit shall fall
  Sudden from heaven like a weeping cloud,
That fosters the droop-headed flowers all,
  And hides the green hill in an April shroud;
Then glut thy sorrow on a morning rose.
  Or on the rainbow of the salt sand-wave,
    Or on the wealth of globed peonies;
Or if thy mistress some rich anger shows,
  Emprison her soft hand, and let her rave,
    And feed deep, deep upon her peerless eyes.

She dwells with Beauty—Beauty that must die;
  And Joy, whose hand is ever at his lips
Bidding adieu; and aching Pleasure nigh,
  Turning to poison while the bee-mouth sips:
Ay, in the very temple of Delight
  Veil'd Melancholy has her sovran shrine,
    Though seen of none save him whose strenuous tongue
  Can burst Joy's grape against his palate fine;
His soul shall taste the sadness of her might,
    And be among her cloudy trophies hung.

ODE TO PSYCHE

O Goddess! hear these tuneless numbers, wrung
By sweet enforcement and remembrance dear,
And pardon that thy secrets should be sung
Even into thine own soft-conched ear:
Surely I dreamt today, or did I see
The winged Psyche with awakened eyes?
I wandered in a forest thoughtlessly,
And, on the sudden, fainting with surprise,
Saw two fair creatures, couched side by side
In deepest grass, beneath the whisp'ring roof
Of leaves and trembled blossoms, where there ran
A brooklet, scarce espied:
'Mid hushed, cool-rooted flowers, fragrant-eyed,
Blue, silver-white, and budded Tyrian,
They lay calm-breathing on the bedded grass;
Their arms embraced, and their pinions too;
Their lips touched not, but had not bade adieu,
As if disjoined by soft-handed slumber,
And ready still past kisses to outnumber
At tender eye-dawn of aurorean love:
The winged boy I knew;
But who wast thou, O happy, happy dove?

His Psyche true!
O latest born and loveliest vision far
Of all Olympus' faded hierarchy!
Fairer than Phoebe's sapphire-regioned star,
Or Vesper, amorous glow-worm of the sky;
Fairer than these, though temple thou hast none,
Nor altar heaped with flowers;
Nor virgin-choir to make delicious moan
Upon the midnight hours;
No voice, no lute, no pipe, no incense sweet
From chain-swung censer teeming;
No shrine, no grove, no oracle, no heat
Of pale-mouthed prophet dreaming.
O brightest! though too late for antique vows,
Too, too late for the fond believing lyre,
When holy were the haunted forest boughs,
Holy the air, the water, and the fire;
Yet even in these days so far retired
From happy pieties, thy lucent fans,
Fluttering among the faint Olympians,
I see, and sing, by my own eyes inspired.
So let me be thy choir, and make a moan
Upon the midnight hours;
Thy voice, thy lute, thy pipe, thy incense sweet
From swinged censer teeming;
Thy shrine, thy grove, thy oracle, thy heat
Of pale-mouthed prophet dreaming.
Yes, I will be thy priest, and build a fane
In some untrodden region of my mind,
Where branched thoughts, new grown with pleasant pain,
Instead of pines shall murmur in the wind:
Far, far around shall those dark-clustered trees
Fledge the wild-ridged mountains steep by steep;
And there by zephyrs, streams, and birds, and bees,
The moss-lain dryads shall be lulled to sleep;
And in the midst of this wide quietness
A rosy sanctuary will I dress

With the wreathed trellis of a working brain,
With buds, and bells, and stars without a name,
With all the gardener Fancy e'er could feign,
Who breeding flowers, will never breed the same:
And there shall be for thee all soft delight
That shadowy thought can win,
A bright torch, and a casement ope at night,
To let the warm Love in!

THE EVE OF ST. AGNES

I.

St. Agnes' Eve——Ah, bitter chill it was!
The owl, for all his feathers, was a-cold;
The hare limp'd trembling through the frozen grass,
And silent was the flock in woolly fold:
Numb were the Beadsman's fingers, while he told
His rosary, and while his frosted breath,
Like pious incense from a censer old,
Seem'd taking flight for heaven, without a death,
Past the sweet Virgin's picture, while his prayer he saith.

II.

His prayer he saith, this patient, holy man;
Then takes his lamp, and riseth from his knees,
And back returneth, meagre, barefoot, wan,
Along the chapel aisle by slow degrees:
The sculptur'd dead, on each side, seem to freeze,
Emprison'd in black, purgatorial rails:
Knights, ladies, praying in dumb orat'ries,
He passeth by; and his weak spirit fails

To think how they may ache in icy hoods and mails.

III.

> Northward he turneth through a little door,
> And scarce three steps, ere Music's golden tongue
> Flatter'd to tears this aged man and poor;
> But no——already had his deathbell rung;
> The joys of all his life were said and sung:
> His was harsh penance on St. Agnes' Eve:
> Another way he went, and soon among
> Rough ashes sat he for his soul's reprieve,
> And all night kept awake, for sinners' sake to grieve.

IV.

> That ancient Beadsman heard the prelude soft;
> And so it chanc'd, for many a door was wide,
> From hurry to and fro. Soon, up aloft,
> The silver, snarling trumpets 'gan to chide:
> The level chambers, ready with their pride,
> Were glowing to receive a thousand guests:
> The carved angels, ever eager-eyed,
> Star'd, where upon their heads the cornice rests,
> With hair blown back, and wings put cross-wise on their
> breasts.

V.

> At length burst in the argent revelry,
> With plume, tiara, and all rich array,
> Numerous as shadows haunting fairily
> The brain, new stuff d, in youth, with triumphs gay
> Of old romance. These let us wish away,
> And turn, sole-thoughted, to one Lady there,
> Whose heart had brooded, all that wintry day,
> On love, and wing'd St. Agnes' saintly care,

As she had heard old dames full many times declare.

VI.

They told her how, upon St. Agnes' Eve,
Young virgins might have visions of delight,
And soft adorings from their loves receive
Upon the honey'd middle of the night,
If ceremonies due they did aright;
As, supperless to bed they must retire,
And couch supine their beauties, lily white;
Nor look behind, nor sideways, but require
Of Heaven with upward eyes for all that they desire.

VII.

Full of this whim was thoughtful Madeline:
The music, yearning like a God in pain,
She scarcely heard: her maiden eyes divine,
Fix'd on the floor, saw many a sweeping train
Pass by——she heeded not at all: in vain
Came many a tiptoe, amorous cavalier,
And back retir'd; not cool'd by high disdain,
But she saw not: her heart was otherwhere:
She sigh'd for Agnes' dreams, the sweetest of the year.

VIII.

She danc'd along with vague, regardless eyes,
Anxious her lips, her breathing quick and short:
The hallow'd hour was near at hand: she sighs
Amid the timbrels, and the throng'd resort
Of whisperers in anger, or in sport;
'Mid looks of love, defiance, hate, and scorn,
Hoodwink'd with faery fancy; all amort,
Save to St. Agnes and her lambs unshorn,
And all the bliss to be before to-morrow morn.

IX.

So, purposing each moment to retire,
She linger'd still. Meantime, across the moors,
Had come young Porphyro, with heart on fire
For Madeline. Beside the portal doors,
Buttress'd from moonlight, stands he, and implores
All saints to give him sight of Madeline,
But for one moment in the tedious hours,
That he might gaze and worship all unseen;
Perchance speak, kneel, touch, kiss—in sooth such things
have been.

X.

He ventures in: let no buzz'd whisper tell:
All eyes be muffled, or a hundred swords
Will storm his heart, Love's fev'rous citadel:
For him, those chambers held barbarian hordes,
Hyena foemen, and hot-blooded lords,
Whose very dogs would execrations howl
Against his lineage: not one breast affords
Him any mercy, in that mansion foul,
Save one old beldame, weak in body and in soul.

XI.

Ah, happy chance! the aged creature came,
Shuffling along with ivory-headed wand,
To where he stood, hid from the torch's flame,
Behind a broad hall-pillar, far beyond
The sound of merriment and chorus bland:
He startled her; but soon she knew his face,
And grasp'd his fingers in her palsied hand,
Saying, "Mercy, Porphyro! hie thee from this place;
"They are all here to-night, the whole blood-thirsty race!

XII.

"Get hence! get hence! there's dwarfish Hildebrand;
"He had a fever late, and in the fit
"He cursed thee and thine, both house and land:
"Then there 's that old Lord Maurice, not a whit
"More tame for his gray hairs——Alas me! flit!
"Flit like a ghost away."——"Ah, Gossip dear,
"We're safe enough; here in this arm-chair sit,
"And tell me how"——"Good Saints! not here, not here;
"Follow me, child, or else these stones will be thy bier."

XIII.

He follow'd through a lowly arched way,
Brushing the cobwebs with his lofty plume;
And as she mutter'd "Well-a——well-a-day!"
He found him in a little moonlight room,
Pale, lattic'd, chill, and silent as a tomb.
"Now tell me where is Madeline," said he,
"O tell me, Angela, by the holy loom
"Which none but secret sisterhood may see,
"When they St. Agnes' wool are weaving piously."

XIV.

"St. Agnes! Ah! it is St. Agnes' Eve——
"Yet men will murder upon holy days:
"Thou must hold water in a witch's sieve,
"And be liege-lord of all the Elves and Fays,
"To venture so: it fills me with amaze
"To see thee, Porphyro!——St. Agnes' Eve!
"God's help! my lady fair the conjuror plays
"This very night: good angels her deceive!
"But let me laugh awhile, I've mickle time to grieve."

XV.

Feebly she laugheth in the languid moon,
While Porphyro upon her face doth look,
Like puzzled urchin on an aged crone
Who keepeth clos'd a wond'rous riddle-book,
As spectacled she sits in chimney nook.
But soon his eyes grew brilliant, when she told
His lady's purpose; and he scarce could brook
Tears, at the thought of those enchantments cold,
And Madeline asleep in lap of legends old.

XVI.

Sudden a thought came like a full-blown rose,
Flushing his brow, and in his pained heart
Made purple riot: then doth he propose
A stratagem, that makes the beldame start:
"A cruel man and impious thou art:
"Sweet lady, let her pray, and sleep, and dream
"Alone with her good angels, far apart
"From wicked men like thee. Go, go!—I deem
"Thou canst not surely be the same that thou didst seem.

XVII.

"I will not harm her, by all saints I swear,"
Quoth Porphyro: "O may I ne'er find grace
"When my weak voice shall whisper its last prayer,
"If one of her soft ringlets I displace,
"Or look with ruffian passion in her face:
"Good Angela, believe me by these tears;
"Or I will, even in a moment's space,
"Awake, with horrid shout, my foemen's ears,
"And beard them, though they be more fang'd than wolves
and bears."

XVIII.

"Ah! why wilt thou affright a feeble soul?
"A poor, weak, palsy-stricken, churchyard thing,
"Whose passing-bell may ere the midnight toll;
"Whose prayers for thee, each morn and evening,
"Were never miss'd."——Thus plaining, doth she bring
A gentler speech from burning Porphyro;
So woful, and of such deep sorrowing,
That Angela gives promise she will do
Whatever he shall wish, betide her weal or woe.

XIX.

Which was, to lead him, in close secrecy,
Even to Madeline's chamber, and there hide
Him in a closet, of such privacy
That he might see her beauty unespied,
And win perhaps that night a peerless bride,
While legion'd fairies pac'd the coverlet,
And pale enchantment held her sleepy-eyed.
Never on such a night have lovers met,
Since Merlin paid his Demon all the monstrous debt.

XX.

"It shall be as thou wishest," said the Dame:
"All cates and dainties shall be stored there
"Quickly on this feast-night: by the tambour frame
"Her own lute thou wilt see: no time to spare,
"For I am slow and feeble, and scarce dare
"On such a catering trust my dizzy head.
"Wait here, my child, with patience; kneel in prayer
"The while: Ah! thou must needs the lady wed,
"Or may I never leave my grave among the dead."

XXI.

So saying, she hobbled off with busy fear.
The lover's endless minutes slowly pass'd;
The dame return'd, and whisper'd in his ear
To follow her; with aged eyes aghast
From fright of dim espial. Safe at last,
Through many a dusky gallery, they gain
The maiden's chamber, silken, hush'd, and chaste;
Where Porphyro took covert, pleas'd amain.
His poor guide hurried back with agues in her brain.

XXII.

Her falt'ring hand upon the balustrade,
Old Angela was feeling for the stair,
When Madeline, St. Agnes' charmed maid,
Rose, like a mission'd spirit, unaware:
With silver taper's light, and pious care,
She turn'd, and down the aged gossip led
To a safe level matting. Now prepare,
Young Porphyro, for gazing on that bed;
She comes, she comes again, like ring-dove fray'd and fled.

XXIII.

Out went the taper as she hurried in;
Its little smoke, in pallid moonshine, died:
She clos'd the door, she panted, all akin
To spirits of the air, and visions wide:
No uttered syllable, or, woe betide!
But to her heart, her heart was voluble,
Paining with eloquence her balmy side;
As though a tongueless nightingale should swell
Her throat in vain, and die, heart-stifled, in her dell.

XXIV.

A casement high and triple-arch'd there was,
All garlanded with carven imag'ries
Of fruits, and flowers, and bunches of knot-grass,
And diamonded with panes of quaint device,
Innumerable of stains and splendid dyes,
As are the tiger-moth's deep-damask'd wings;
And in the midst, 'mong thousand heraldries,
And twilight saints, and dim emblazonings,
A shielded scutcheon blush'd with blood of queens and
kings.

XXV.

Full on this casement shone the wintry moon,
And threw warm gules on Madeline's fair breast,
As down she knelt for heaven's grace and boon;
Rose-bloom fell on her hands, together prest,
And on her silver cross soft amethyst,
And on her hair a glory, like a saint:
She seem'd a splendid angel, newly drest,
Save wings, for heaven:——Porphyro grew faint:
She knelt, so pure a thing, so free from mortal taint.

XXVI.

Anon his heart revives: her vespers done,
Of all its wreathed pearls her hair she frees;
Unclasps her warmed jewels one by one;
Loosens her fragrant boddice; by degrees
Her rich attire creeps rustling to her knees:
Half-hidden, like a mermaid in sea-weed,
Pensive awhile she dreams awake, and sees,
In fancy, fair St. Agnes in her bed,
But dares not look behind, or all the charm is fled.

XXVII.

Soon, trembling in her soft and chilly nest,
In sort of wakeful swoon, perplex'd she lay,
Until the poppied warmth of sleep oppress'd
Her soothed limbs, and soul fatigued away;
Flown, like a thought, until the morrow-day;
Blissfully haven'd both from joy and pain;
Clasp'd like a missal where swart Paynims pray;
Blinded alike from sunshine and from rain,
As though a rose should shut, and be a bud again.

XXVIII.

Stol'n to this paradise, and so entranced,
Porphyro gazed upon her empty dress,
And listen'd to her breathing, if it chanced
To wake into a slumberous tenderness;
Which when he heard, that minute did he bless,
And breath'd himself: then from the closet crept,
Noiseless as fear in a wide wilderness,
And over the hush'd carpet, silent, stept,
And 'tween the curtains peep'd, where, lo!——how fast she
slept.

XXIX.

Then by the bed-side, where the faded moon
Made a dim, silver twilight, soft he set
A table, and, half anguish'd, threw thereon
A cloth of woven crimson, gold, and jet:——
O for some drowsy Morphean amulet!
The boisterous, midnight, festive clarion,
The kettle-drum, and far-heard clarionet,
Affray his ears, though but in dying tone:——
The hall door shuts again, and all the noise is gone.

XXX.

And still she slept an azure-lidded sleep,
In blanched linen, smooth, and lavender'd,
While he from forth the closet brought a heap
Of candied apple, quince, and plum, and gourd;
With jellies soother than the creamy curd,
And lucent syrops, tinct with cinnamon;
Manna and dates, in argosy transferr'd
From Fez; and spiced dainties, every one,
From silken Samarcand to cedar'd Lebanon.

XXXI.

These delicates he heap'd with glowing hand
On golden dishes and in baskets bright
Of wreathed silver: sumptuous they stand
In the retired quiet of the night,
Filling the chilly room with perfume light.——
"And now, my love, my seraph fair, awake!
"Thou art my heaven, and I thine eremite:
"Open thine eyes, for meek St. Agnes' sake,
"Or I shall drowse beside thee, so my soul doth ache."

XXXII.

Thus whispering, his warm, unnerved arm
Sank in her pillow. Shaded was her dream
By the dusk curtains:——'twas a midnight charm
Impossible to melt as iced stream:
The lustrous salvers in the moonlight gleam;
Broad golden fringe upon the carpet lies:
It seem'd he never, never could redeem
From such a stedfast spell his lady's eyes;
So mus'd awhile, entoil'd in woofed phantasies.

XXXIII.

Awakening up, he took her hollow lute,——

Tumultuous,——and, in chords that tenderest be,
He play'd an ancient ditty, long since mute,
In Provence call'd, "La belle dame sans mercy:"
Close to her ear touching the melody;——
Wherewith disturb'd, she utter'd a soft moan:
He ceased——she panted quick——and suddenly
Her blue affrayed eyes wide open shone:
Upon his knees he sank, pale as smooth-sculptured stone.

XXXIV.

Her eyes were open, but she still beheld,
Now wide awake, the vision of her sleep:
There was a painful change, that nigh expell'd
The blisses of her dream so pure and deep
At which fair Madeline began to weep,
And moan forth witless words with many a sigh;
While still her gaze on Porphyro would keep;
Who knelt, with joined hands and piteous eye,
Fearing to move or speak, she look'd so dreamingly.

XXXV.

"Ah, Porphyro!" said she, "but even now
"Thy voice was at sweet tremble in mine ear,
"Made tuneable with every sweetest vow;
"And those sad eyes were spiritual and clear:
"How chang'd thou art! how pallid, chill, and drear!
"Give me that voice again, my Porphyro,
"Those looks immortal, those complainings dear!
"Oh leave me not in this eternal woe,
"For if thou diest, my Love, I know not where to go."

XXXVI.

Beyond a mortal man impassion'd far
At these voluptuous accents, he arose,

Ethereal, flush'd, and like a throbbing star
Seen mid the sapphire heaven's deep repose;
Into her dream he melted, as the rose
Blendeth its odour with the violet,—
Solution sweet: meantime the frost-wind blows
Like Love's alarum pattering the sharp sleet
Against the window-panes; St. Agnes' moon hath set.

XXXVII.

'Tis dark: quick pattereth the flaw-blown sleet:
"This is no dream, my bride, my Madeline!"
'Tis dark: the iced gusts still rave and beat:
"No dream, alas! alas! and woe is mine!
"Porphyro will leave me here to fade and pine.—
"Cruel! what traitor could thee hither bring?
"I curse not, for my heart is lost in thine,
"Though thou forsakest a deceived thing;—
"A dove forlorn and lost with sick unpruned wing."

XXXVIII.

"My Madeline! sweet dreamer! lovely bride!
"Say, may I be for aye thy vassal blest?
"Thy beauty's shield, heart-shap'd and vermeil dyed?
"Ah, silver shrine, here will I take my rest
"After so many hours of toil and quest,
"A famish'd pilgrim,—saved by miracle.
"Though I have found, I will not rob thy nest
"Saving of thy sweet self; if thou think'st well
"To trust, fair Madeline, to no rude infidel."

XXXIX.

'Hark! 'tis an elfin-storm from faery land,
"Of haggard seeming, but a boon indeed:
"Arise—arise! the morning is at hand;—

"The bloated wassaillers will never heed:——
"Let us away, my love, with happy speed;
"There are no ears to hear, or eyes to see,——
"Drown'd all in Rhenish and the sleepy mead:
"Awake! arise! my love, and fearless be,
"For o'er the southern moors I have a home for thee."

XL.

She hurried at his words, beset with fears,
For there were sleeping dragons all around,
At glaring watch, perhaps, with ready spears——
Down the wide stairs a darkling way they found.——
In all the house was heard no human sound.
A chain-droop'd lamp was flickering by each door;
The arras, rich with horseman, hawk, and hound,
Flutter'd in the besieging wind's uproar;
And the long carpets rose along the gusty floor.

XLI.

They glide, like phantoms, into the wide hall;
Like phantoms, to the iron porch, they glide;
Where lay the Porter, in uneasy sprawl,
With a huge empty flaggon by his side;
The wakeful bloodhound rose, and shook his hide,
But his sagacious eye an inmate owns:
By one, and one, the bolts full easy slide:——
The chains lie silent on the footworn stones;——
The key turns, and the door upon its hinges groans.

XLII.

And they are gone: ay, ages long ago
These lovers fled away into the storm.
That night the Baron dreamt of many a woe,
And all his warrior-guests, with shade and form

Of witch, and demon, and large coffin-worm,
Were long be-nightmar'd. Angela the old
Died palsy-twitch'd, with meagre face deform;
The Beadsman, after thousand aves told,
For aye unsought for slept among his ashes cold.

A DREAM, AFTER READING DANTE'S EPISODE OF PAOLA AND FRANCESCA

As Hermes once took to his feathers light,
  When lulled Argus, baffled, swoone'd and slept,
So on a Delphic reed, my idle spright
  So play'd, so charm'd, so conquer'd, so bereft
The dragon-world of all its hundred eyes;
  And, seeing it asleep, so fled away -
Not to pure Ida with its snow-cold skies,
  Nor unto Tempe where Jove griev'd a day;
But to that second circle of sad hell,
  Where 'mid the gust, the whirlwind, and the flaw
Of rain and hail-stones, lovers need not tell
  Their sorrows. Pale were the sweet lips I saw,
Pale were the lips I kiss'd, and fair the form
I floated with, about that melancholy storm.

TO HOPE

When by my solitary hearth I sit,
  And hateful thoughts enwrap my soul in gloom;
When no fair dreams before my 'mind's eye' flit,
  And the bare heath of life presents no bloom;
    Sweet Hope, ethereal balm upon me shed,
    And wave thy silver pinions o'er my head.

Whene'er I wander, at the fall of night,
  Where woven boughs shut out the moon's bright ray,
Should sad Despondency my musings fright,
  And frown, to drive fair Cheerfulness away,
    Peep with the moon-beams through the leafy roof,
    And keep that fiend Despondence far aloof.

Should Disappointment, parent of Despair,
  Strive for her son to seize my careless heart;
When, like a cloud, he sits upon the air,
  Preparing on his spell-bound prey to dart:
    Chase him away, sweet Hope, with visage bright,
    And fright him as the morning frightens night!

Whene'er the fate of those I hold most dear

Tells to my fearful breast a tale of sorrow,
O bright-eyed Hope, my morbid fancy cheer;
 Let me awhile thy sweetest comforts borrow:
  Thy heaven-born radiance around me shed,
  And wave thy silver pinions o'er my head!

Should e'er unhappy love my bosom pain,
 From cruel parents, or relentless fair;
O let me think it is not quite in vain
 To sigh out sonnets to the midnight air!
  Sweet Hope, ethereal balm upon me shed,
  And wave thy silver pinions o'er my head!

In the long vista of the years to roll,
 Let me not see our country's honour fade:
O let me see our land retain her soul,
 Her pride, her freedom; and not freedom's shade.
  From thy bright eyes unusual brightness shed -
  Beneath thy pinions canopy my head!

Let me not see the patriot's high bequest,
 Great Liberty! how great in plain attire!
With the base purple of a court oppressed,
 Bowing her head, and ready to expire:
  But let me see thee stoop from heaven on wings
  That fill the skies with silver glitterings!

And as, in sparkling majesty, a star
 Gilds the bright summit of some gloomy cloud;
Brightening the half veiled face of heaven afar:
 So, when dark thoughts my boding spirit shroud,
  Sweet Hope, celestial influence round me shed,
  Waving thy silver pinions o'er my head.

A SONG ABOUT MYSELF

I
There was a naughty Boy,
A naughty boy was he,
He would not stop at home,
He could not quiet be -
He took
In his Knapsack
A Book
Full of vowels
And a shirt
With some towels -
A slight cap
For night cap -
A hair brush,
Comb ditto,
New Stockings
For old ones
Would split O!
This Knapsack
Tight at's back
He rivetted close
And followed his Nose

To the North,
To the North,
And follow'd his nose
To the North.
II
There was a naughty boy
And a naughty boy was he,
For nothing would he do
But scribble poetry -
He took
An ink stand
In his hand
And a pen
Big as ten
In the other,
And away
In a Pother
He ran
To the mountains
And fountains
And ghostes
And Postes
And witches
And ditches
And wrote
In his coat
When the weather
Was cool,
Fear of gout,
And without
When the weather
Was warm -
Och the charm
When we choose
To follow one's nose
To the north,
To the north,

To follow one's nose
To the north!
III
There was a naughty boy
And a naughty boy was he,
He kept little fishes
In washing tubs three
In spite
Of the might
Of the maid
Nor afraid
Of his Granny-good-
He often would
Hurly burly
Get up early
And go
By hook or crook
To the brook
And bring home
Miller's thumb,
Tittlebat
Not over fat,
Minnows small
As the stall
Of a glove,
Not above
The size
Of a nice
Little Baby's
Little fingers-
O he made
'Twas his trade
Of Fish a pretty Kettle
A Kettle-
A Kettle
Of Fish a pretty Kettle
A Kettle!

IV

There was a naughty Boy,
  And a naughty Boy was he,
He ran away to Scotland
  The people for to see -
    There he found
    That the ground
    Was as hard,
    That a yard
    Was as long,
    That a song
    Was as merry,
    That a cherry
    Was as red -
    That lead
    Was as weighty,
    That fourscore
    Was as eighty,
    That a door
    Was as wooden
    As in England -
So he stood in his shoes
  And he wonder'd,
  He wonder'd,
He stood in his shoes
  And he wonder'd.

THE DAY IS GONE, AND ALL ITS SWEETS ARE GONE

The day is gone, and all its sweets are gone!
Sweet voice, sweet lips, soft hand, and softer breast,
Warm breath, light whisper, tender semitone,
Bright eyes, accomplished shape, and lang'rous waist!
Faded the flower and all its budded charms,
Faded the sight of beauty from my eyes,
Faded the shape of beauty from my arms,
Faded the voice, warmth, whiteness, paradise -
Vanished unseasonably at shut of eve,
When the dusk holiday -or holinight
Of fragrant-curtained love begins to weave
The woof of darkness thick, for hid delight;
But, as I've read love's missal through today,
He'll let me sleep, seeing I fast and pray.

TO A YOUNG LADY WHO SENT ME A LAUREL CROWN

Fresh morning gusts have blown away all fear
  From my glad bosom - now from gloominess
  I mount for ever - not an atom less
Than the proud laurel shall content my bier.
No! by the eternal stars! or why sit here
  In the Sun's eye, and 'gainst my temples press
  Apollo's very leaves, woven to bless
By thy white fingers and thy spirit clear.
Lo! who dares say, "Do this"? Who dares call down
  My will from its high purpose? Who say,"Stand,"
Or, "Go"? This mighty moment I would frown
  On abject Caesars - not the stoutest band
Of mailed heroes should tear off my crown:
  Yet would I kneel and kiss thy gentle hand.

ODE TO APOLLO

In thy western halls of gold
   When thou sittest in thy state,
Bards, that erst sublimely told
   Heroic deeds, and sung of fate,
With fervour seize their adamantine lyres,
Whose chords are solid rays, and twinkle radiant fires.

There Homer with his nervous arms
   Strikes the twanging harp of war,
And even the western splendour warms,
   While the trumpets sound afar:
But, what creates the most intense surprise,
His soul looks out through renovated eyes.

Then, through thy Temple wide, melodious swells
   The sweet majestic tone of Maro's lyre:
The soul delighted on each accent dwells, -
   Enraptur'd dwells, - not daring to respire,
The while he tells of grief around a funeral pyre.

'Tis awful silence then again;
   Expectant stand the spheres;

Breathless the laurelled peers,
Nor move, till ends the lofty strain,
Nor move till Milton's tuneful thunders cease,
And leave once more the ravished heavens in peace.

Thou biddest Shakespeare wave his hand,
And quickly forward spring
The Passions - a terrific band -
And each vibrates the string
That with its tyrant temper best accords,
While from their Master's lips pour forth the inspiring
words.

A silver trumpet Spenser blows,
And, as its martial notes to silence flee,
From a virgin chorus flows
A hymn in praise of spotless Chastity.
'Tis still! Wild warblings from the Aeolian lyre
Enchantment softly breathe, and tremblingly expire.

Next thy Tasso's ardent numbers
Float along the pleasèd air,
Calling youth from idle slumbers,
Rousing them from Pleasure's lair: -
Then o'er the strings his fingers gently move,
And melt the soul to pity and to love.

But when Thou joinest with the Nine,
And all the powers of song combine,
We listen here on earth:
Thy dying tones that fill the air,
And charm the ear of evening fair,
From thee, great God of Bards, receive their heavenly birth.

AS FROM THE DARKENING GLOOM A
SILVER DOVE

As from the darkening gloom a silver dove
  Upsoars, and darts into the Eastern light,
  On pinions that naught moves but pure delight;
So fled thy soul into the realms above,
Regions of peace and everlasting love;
  Where happy spirits, crowned with circlets bright
  Of starry beam, and gloriously bedight,
Taste the high joy none but the blest can prove.
There thou or joinest the immortal quire
  In melodies that even Heaven fair
Fill with superior bliss, or, at desire
  Of the omnipotent Father, cleavest the air,
On holy message sent - What pleasures higher?
  Wherefore does any grief our joy impair?

ON PEACE

O Peace! and dost thou with thy presence bless
  The dwellings of this war-surrounded Isle;
Soothing with placid brow our late distress,
  Making the triple kingdom brightly smile?
Joyful I hail thy presence; and I hail
  The sweet companions that await on thee;
Complete my joy - let not my first wish fail,
  Let the sweet mountain nymph thy favourite be,
With England's happiness proclaim Europa's liberty.
O Europe! Let not sceptred tyrants see
  That thou must shelter in thy former state;
Keep thy chains burst, and boldy say thou art free;
  Give thy kings law - leave not uncurbed the great;
  So with the horrors past thou'lt win thy happier fate!

OH HOW I LOVE, ON A FAIR SUMMER'S EVE

Oh! how I love, on a fair summer's eve,
  When streams of light pour down the golden west,
  And on the balmy zephyrs tranquil rest
The silver clouds, -- far, far away to leave
All meaner thoughts, and take a sweet reprieve
  From little cares; to find, with easy quest,
  A fragrant wild, with Nature's beauty drest,
And there into delight my soul deceive.
There warm my breast with patriotic lore,
  Musing on Milton's fate -- on Sydney's bier --
  Till their stern forms before my mind arise:
Perhaps on the wing of Poesy upsoar,
  Full often dropping a delicious tear,
  When some melodious sorrow spells mine eyes.

O SOLITUDE! IF I MUST WITH THEE DWELL

O Solitude! if I must with thee dwell,
   Let it not be among the jumbled heap
   Of murky buildings; climb with me the steep, —
Nature's observatory — whence the dell,
Its flowery slopes, its river's crystal swell,
   May seem a span; let me thy vigils keep
   'Mongst boughs pavillion'd, where the deer's swift leap
Startles the wild bee from the fox-glove bell.
But though I'll gladly trace these scenes with thee, [1]
   Yet the sweet converse of an innocent mind,
   Whose words are images of thoughts refin'd,
Is my soul's pleasure; and it sure must be
   Almost the highest bliss of human-kind,
When to thy haunts two kindred spirits flee.

ON LEAVING SOME FRIENDS AT AN EARLY HOUR

Give me a golden pen, and let me lean
  On heaped-up flowers, in regions clear, and far;
  Bring me a tablet whiter than a star,
Or hand of hymning angel, when 'tis seen
The silver strings of heavenly harp atween:
  And let there glide by many a pearly car
  Pink robes, and wavy hair, and diamond jar,
And half-discovered wings, and glances keen.
The while let music wander round my ears,
And as it reaches each delicious ending,
Let me write down a line of glorious tone,
And full of many wonders of the spheres:
For what a height my spirit is contending!
'Tis not content so soon to be alone.

WHEN I HAVE FEARS THAT I MAY CEASE TO BE

When I have fears that I may cease to be
Before my pen has glean'd my teeming brain,
Before high piled books, in charactry,
Hold like rich garners the full ripen'd grain;
When I behold, upon the night's starr'd face,
Huge cloudy symbols of a high romance,
And think that I may never live to trace
Their shadows, with the magic hand of chance;
And when I feel, fair creature of an hour,
That I shall never look upon thee more,
Never have relish in the fairy power
Of unreflecting love;—then on the shore
Of the wide world I stand alone, and think
Till love and fame to nothingness do sink.

FANCY

Ever let the Fancy roam,
Pleasure never is at home:
At a touch sweet Pleasure melteth,
Like to bubbles when rain pelteth;
Then let winged Fancy wander
Through the thought still spread beyond her:
Open wide the mind's cage-door,
She'll dart forth, and cloudward soar.
O sweet Fancy! let her loose;
Summer's joys are spoilt by use,
And the enjoying of the Spring
Fades as does its blossoming;
Autumn's red-lipp'd fruitage too,
Blushing through the mist and dew,
Cloys with tasting: What do then?
Sit thee by the ingle, when
The sear faggot blazes bright,
Spirit of a winter's night;
When the soundless earth is muffled,
And the caked snow is shuffled
From the ploughboy's heavy shoon;
When the Night doth meet the Noon

In a dark conspiracy
To banish Even from her sky.
Sit thee there, and send abroad,
With a mind self-overaw'd,
Fancy, high-commission'd:—send her!
She has vassals to attend her:
She will bring, in spite of frost,
Beauties that the earth hath lost;
She will bring thee, all together,
All delights of summer weather;
All the buds and bells of May,
From dewy sward or thorny spray
All the heaped Autumn's wealth,
With a still, mysterious stealth:
She will mix these pleasures up
Like three fit wines in a cup,
And thou shalt quaff it:—thou shalt hear
Distant harvest-carols clear;
Rustle of the reaped corn;
Sweet birds antheming the morn:
And, in the same moment—hark!
'Tis the early April lark,
Or the rooks, with busy caw,
Foraging for sticks and straw.
Thou shalt, at one glance, behold
The daisy and the marigold;
White-plum'd lilies, and the first
Hedge-grown primrose that hath burst;
Shaded hyacinth, alway
Sapphire queen of the mid-May;
And every leaf, and every flower
Pearled with the self-same shower.
Thou shalt see the field-mouse peep
Meagre from its celled sleep;
And the snake all winter-thin
Cast on sunny bank its skin;
Freckled nest-eggs thou shalt see

Hatching in the hawthorn-tree,
When the hen-bird's wing doth rest
Quiet on her mossy nest;
Then the hurry and alarm
When the bee-hive casts its swarm;
Acorns ripe down-pattering,
While the autumn breezes sing.
Oh, sweet Fancy! let her loose;
Every thing is spoilt by use:
Where's the cheek that doth not fade,
Too much gaz'd at? Where's the maid
Whose lip mature is ever new?
Where's the eye, however blue,
Doth not weary? Where's the face
One would meet in every place?
Where's the voice, however soft,
One would hear so very oft?
At a touch sweet Pleasure melteth
Like to bubbles when rain pelteth.
Let, then, winged Fancy find
Thee a mistress to thy mind:
Dulcet-eyed as Ceres' daughter,
Ere the God of Torment taught her
How to frown and how to chide;
With a waist and with a side
White as Hebe's, when her zone
Slipt its golden clasp, and down
Fell her kirtle to her feet,
While she held the goblet sweet,
And Jove grew languid.—Break the mesh
Of the Fancy's silken leash;
Quickly break her prison-string
And such joys as these she'll bring.—
Let the winged Fancy roam
Pleasure never is at home.

GOD OF THE MERIDIAN

God of the meridian!
  And of the east and west!
To thee my soul is flown,
  And my body is earthward press'd:
It is an awful mission,
A terrible division,
And leaves a gulf austere
To be fill'd with worldly fear.
Aye, when the soul is fled
Too high above our head,
Affrighted do we gaze
After its airy maze –
As doth a mother wild
When her young infant child
Is in an eagle's claws.
And is not this the cause
Of madness? – God of Song,
Thou bearest me along
Through sights I scarce can bear;
O let me, let me share
With the hot lyre and thee
The staid philosophy.

Temper my lonely hours
And let me see thy bowers
    More unalarmed! * * *

THE HUMAN SEASONS

Four seasons fill the measure of the year ;
There are four seasons in the mind of man.
He has his lusty Spring, when fancy clear
Takes in all beauty with an easy span.
He has his Summer, when luxuriously
Spring's honeyed cud of youthful thought he loves
To ruminate, and by such dreaming nigh
His nearest unto heaven. Quiet coves
His soul has its Autumn, when his wings
He furleth close ; contented so to look
On mists in idleness - to let fair things
Pass by unheeded as a thresold brook.
He has his Winter too of pale misfeature,
Or else he would forego his mortal nature.

FAERY SONGS

I

Shed no tear! O shed no tear!
The flower will bloom another year.
Weep no more! O weep no more!
Young buds sleep in the root's white core.
Dry your eyes! O dry your eyes,
For I was taught in Paradise
To ease my breast of melodies —
       Shed no tear.

Overhead! look overhead
'Mong the blossoms white and red —
Look up, look up — I flutter now
On this flush pomegranate bough.
See me! 't is this silvery bill
Ever cures the good man's ill.
Shed no tear! O shed no tear!
The flower will bloom another year.
Adieu, adieu — I fly, adieu,
I vanish in the heaven's blue —
       Adieu, adieu!

II

Ah! woe is me! poor silver-wing!
  That I must chant thy lady's dirge,
And death to this haunt of spring,
  Of melody, and streams of flowery verge, —
      Poor silver-wing! ah! woe is me!
      That I must see
These blossoms snow upon thy lady's pall!
  Go, pretty page! and in her ear
  Whisper that the hour is near!
  Softly tell her not to fear
Such calm favonian burial!
  Go, pretty page! and soothly tell, —
  The blossoms hang by a melting spell,
And fall they must, ere a star wink thrice
      Upon her closed eyes,
That now in vain are weeping their last tears,
  At sweet life leaving, and those arbours green, —
Rich dowry from the Spirit of the Spheres, —
      Alas! poor Queen!

I CRY YOUR MERCY, PITY, LOVE - AY, LOVE

I cry your mercy — pity — love — ay, love!
Merciful love that tantalizes not,
One-thoughted, never-wandering, guileless love,
Unmask'd, and being seen — without a blot!
O! let me have thee whole, — all — all — be mine!
That shape, that fairness, that sweet minor zest
Of love, your kiss, — those hands, those eyes divine,
That warm, white, lucent, million-pleasured breast, —
Yourself — your soul — in pity give me all,
Withhold no atom's atom, or I die,
Or living on perhaps, your wretched thrall,
Forget, in the mist of idle misery,
Life's purposes — the palate of my mind
Losing its gust, and my ambition blind!

IN DREAR-NIGHTED DECEMBER

In a drear-nighted December,
  Too happy, happy tree,
Thy branches ne'er remember
  Their green felicity;
The north cannot undo them,
With a sleety whistle through them;
Nor frozen thawings glue them
  From budding at the prime.

In a drear-nighted December,
  Too happy, happy brook,
Thy bubblings ne'er remember
  Apollo's summer look;
But with a sweet forgetting,
They stay their crystal fretting,
Never, never petting
  About the frozen time.

Ah! would 'twere so with many
  A gentle girl and boy!
But were there ever any
  Writh'd not at passing joy?

The feel of not to feel it,
Where there is none to heal it,
Nor numbed sense to steal it,
  Was never said in rhyme.

ON THE SEA

It keeps eternal whisperings around
Desolate shores, and with its mighty swell
Gluts twice ten thousand caverns, till the spell
Of Hecate leaves them their old shadowy sound.
Often 'tis in such gentle temper found,
That scarcely will the very smallest shell
Be moved for days from whence it sometime fell,
When last the winds of heaven were unbound.
Oh ye! who have your eye-balls vexed and tired,
Feast them upon the wideness of the Sea;
Oh ye! whose ears are dinned with uproar rude,
Or fed too much with cloying melody, -
Sit ye near some old cavern's mouth, and brood
Until ye start, as if the sea-nymphs choired!

ACROSTIC

Give me your patience, sister, while I frame
Exact in capitals your golden name,
Or sue the fair Apollo, and he will
Rouse from his heavy slumber and instill
Great love in me for thee and Poesy.
Imagine not that greatest mastery
And kingdom over all the realms of verse,
Nears more to heaven in aught than when we nurse
And surety give, to love and Brotherhood.

Anthropophagi in Othello's mood,
Ulysses stormed and his enchanted belt
Glow with the Muse, but they are never felt
Unbosomed so and so eternal made,
Such tender incense in their laurel shade,
To all the regent sisters of the Nine,
As this poor offering to you, sister mine.

Kind sister! ay, this third name says you are.
Enchanted has it been the Lord knows where.
And may it taste to you like good old wine,
Take you to real happiness and give
Sons, daughters and a home like honeyed hive.

AND WHAT IS LOVE? IT IS A DOLL DRESSED UP

And what is love? It is a doll dressed up
For idleness to cosset, nurse, and dandle;
A thing of soft misnomers, so divine
That silly youth doth think to make itself
Divine by loving, and so goes on
Yawning and doting a whole summer long,
Till Miss's comb is made a perfect tiara,
And common Wellingtons turn Romeo boots;
Till Cleopatra lives at Number Seven,
And Antony resides in Brunswick Square.
Fools! if some passions high have warmed the world,
If queens and soldiers have played deep for hearts,
It is no reason why such agonies
Should be more common than the growth of weeds.
Fools! make me whole again that weighty pearl
The queen of Egypt melted, and I'll say
That ye may love in spite of beaver hats.

APOLLO TO THE GRACES

APOLLO
    Which of the fairest three
    Today will ride with me?
My steeds are all pawing on the thresholds of Morn:
    Which of the fairest three
    Today will ride with me?
Across the gold Autumn's whole kingdoms of corn?

THE GRACES all answer
    I will, I - I - I -
    O young Apollo let me fly along with thee,
    I will, I - I - I -
      The many, many wonders see -
    I - I - I - I -
And thy lyre shall never have a slackened string.
      I - I - I - I -
Thro' the whole day will sing.

TO FANNY

I cry your mercy—pity—love!—aye, love!
Merciful love that tantalizes not,
One—thoughtèd, never—wandering, guileless love,
Unmasked, and being seen—without a blot!
O! let me have thee whole,—all—all—be mine!
That shape, that fairness, that sweet minor zest
Of love, your kiss,—those hands, those eyes divine,
That warm, white, lucent, million—pleasured breast,—
Yourself—your soul—in pity give me all,
Withhold no atom's atom or I die,
Or living on, perhaps, your wretched thrall,
Forget, in the mist of idle misery,
Life's purposes,—the palate of my mind
Losing its gust, and my ambition blind!—

SWEET, SWEET IS THE GREETING OF EYES

Sweet, sweet is the greetings of the eyes
And sweet is the voice in its greeting.
When adieux have grown old and goodbyes
Fade away when old time is retreating.

Warm the nerve of a welcoming hand
and earnest a kiss on the brow,
When we meet over the sea and o'er land
Where furrows are new to the plough.

THIS LIVING HAND

This living hand, now warm and capable
Of earnest grasping, would, if it were cold
And in the icy silence of the tomb,
So haunt thy days and chill thy dreaming nights
That thou wouldst wish thine own heart dry of blood
So in my veins red life might stream again,
And thou be conscience-calm'd—see here it is—
I hold it towards you.

TO HOMER

Standing aloof in giant ignorance,
Of thee I hear and of the Cyclades,
As one who sits ashore and longs perchance
To visit dolphin-coral in deep seas.
So was thou blind;—but then the veil was rent,
For Jove uncurtain'd heaven to let thee live,
And Neptune made for thee a spumy tent,
And Pan made sing for thee his forest-hive;
Aye on the shores of darkness there is light,
And precipices show untrodden green,
There is a budding morrow in midnight,
There is a triple sight in blindness keen;
Such seeing hadst thou, as it once befel
To Dian, Queen of Earth, and Heaven, and Hell..

HYMN TO APOLLO

God of the golden bow,
And of the golden lyre,
And of the golden hair,
And of the golden fire,
Charioteer
Of the patient year,
Where-where slept thine ire,
When like a blank idiot I put on thy wreath,
Thy laurel, thy glory,
The light of thy story,
Or was I a worm-too low crawling for death?
O Delphic Apollo!

The Thunderer grasp'd and grasp'd,
The Thunderer frown'd and frown'd;
The eagle's feathery mane
For wrath became stiffen'd-the sound
Of breeding thunder
Went drowsily under,
Muttering to be unbound.
O why didst thou pity, and beg for a worm?
Why touch thy soft lute

Till the thunder was mute,
Why was I not crush'd-such a pitiful germ?
O Delphic Apollo!

The Pleiades were up,
Watching the silent air;
The seeds and roots in Earth
Were swelling for summer fare;
The Ocean, its neighbour,
Was at his old labour,
When, who-who did dare
To tie for a moment, thy plant round his brow,
And grin and look proudly,
And blaspheme so loudly,
And live for that honour, to stoop to thee now?
O Delphic Apollo!

OLD MEG SHE WAS A GIPSY

Old Meg she was a Gipsy
And liv'd upon the Moors;
Her bed it was the brown heath turf,
And her house was out of doors.
Her apples were swart blackberries,
Her currants pods o'Broom,
Her wine was dew o' the wild white rose,
Her book a churchyard tomb.
Her brothers were the craggy hills,
Her Sisters larchen trees -
Alone with her great family
She liv'd as she did please.
No Breakfast had she many a morn,
No dinner many a noon;
And 'stead of supper she would stare
Full hard against the Moon.
But every Morn, of wood bine fresh
She made her garlanding;
And every night the dark glen Yew
She wove and she would sing.
And with her fingers old and brown
She plaited Mats o' Rushes,

And gave them to the Cottagers
She met among the Bushes.
Old Meg was brave as Margaret Queen
And tall as Amazon:
An old red blanket cloak she wore
A chip hat had she on -
God rest her aged bones somewhere
She died full long agone!

ISABELLA, OR, THE POT OF BASIL

I.

Fair Isabel, poor simple Isabel!
  Lorenzo, a young palmer in Love's eye!
They could not in the self-same mansion dwell
  Without some stir of heart, some malady;
They could not sit at meals but feel how well
  It soothed each to be the other by;
They could not, sure, beneath the same roof sleep
But to each other dream, and nightly weep.

II.

With every morn their love grew tenderer,
  With every eve deeper and tenderer still;
He might not in house, field, or garden stir,
  But her full shape would all his seeing fill;
And his continual voice was pleasanter
  To her, than noise of trees or hidden rill;
Her lute-string gave an echo of his name,
She spoilt her half-done broidery with the same.

III.

He knew whose gentle hand was at the latch,
  Before the door had given her to his eyes;
And from her chamber-window he would catch

Her beauty farther than the falcon spies;
And constant as her vespers would he watch,
  Because her face was turn'd to the same skies;
And with sick longing all the night outwear,
To hear her morning-step upon the stair.
IV.
A whole long month of May in this sad plight
  Made their cheeks paler by the break of June:
"To morrow will I bow to my delight,
  "To-morrow will I ask my lady's boon."--
"O may I never see another night,
  "Lorenzo, if thy lips breathe not love's tune."--
So spake they to their pillows; but, alas,
Honeyless days and days did he let pass;
V.
Until sweet Isabella's untouch'd cheek
  Fell sick within the rose's just domain,
Fell thin as a young mother's, who doth seek
  By every lull to cool her infant's pain:
"How ill she is," said he, "I may not speak,
  "And yet I will, and tell my love all plain:
"If looks speak love-laws, I will drink her tears,
"And at the least 'twill startle off her cares."
VI.
So said he one fair morning, and all day
  His heart beat awfully against his side;
And to his heart he inwardly did pray
  For power to speak; but still the ruddy tide
Stifled his voice, and puls'd resolve away--
  Fever'd his high conceit of such a bride,
Yet brought him to the meekness of a child:
Alas! when passion is both meek and wild!
VII.
So once more he had wak'd and anguished
  A dreary night of love and misery,
If Isabel's quick eye had not been wed
  To every symbol on his forehead high;

She saw it waxing very pale and dead,
    And straight all flush'd; so, lisped tenderly,
"Lorenzo!"--here she ceas'd her timid quest,
But in her tone and look he read the rest.
VIII.
"O Isabella, I can half perceive
    "That I may speak my grief into thine ear;
"If thou didst ever any thing believe,
    "Believe how I love thee, believe how near
"My soul is to its doom: I would not grieve
    "Thy hand by unwelcome pressing, would not fear
"Thine eyes by gazing; but I cannot live
"Another night, and not my passion shrive.
IX.
"Love! thou art leading me from wintry cold,
    "Lady! thou leadest me to summer clime,
"And I must taste the blossoms that unfold
    "In its ripe warmth this gracious morning time."
So said, his erewhile timid lips grew bold,
    And poesied with hers in dewy rhyme:
Great bliss was with them, and great happiness
Grew, like a lusty flower in June's caress.
X.
Parting they seem'd to tread upon the air,
    Twin roses by the zephyr blown apart
Only to meet again more close, and share
    The inward fragrance of each other's heart.
She, to her chamber gone, a ditty fair
    Sang, of delicious love and honey'd dart;
He with light steps went up a western hill,
And bade the sun farewell, and joy'd his fill.
XI.
All close they met again, before the dusk
    Had taken from the stars its pleasant veil,
All close they met, all eves, before the dusk
    Had taken from the stars its pleasant veil,
Close in a bower of hyacinth and musk,

Unknown of any, free from whispering tale.
Ah! better had it been for ever so,
Than idle ears should pleasure in their woe.
XII.
Were they unhappy then?--It cannot be--
Too many tears for lovers have been shed,
Too many sighs give we to them in fee,
Too much of pity after they are dead,
Too many doleful stories do we see,
Whose matter in bright gold were best be read;
Except in such a page where Theseus' spouse
Over the pathless waves towards him bows.
XIII.
But, for the general award of love,
The little sweet doth kill much bitterness;
Though Dido silent is in under-grove,
And Isabella's was a great distress,
Though young Lorenzo in warm Indian clove
Was not embalm'd, this truth is not the less--
Even bees, the little almsmen of spring-bowers,
Know there is richest juice in poison-flowers.
XIV.
With her two brothers this fair lady dwelt,
Enriched from ancestral merchandize,
And for them many a weary hand did swelt
In torched mines and noisy factories,
And many once proud-quiver'd loins did melt
In blood from stinging whip;--with hollow eyes
Many all day in dazzling river stood,
To take the rich-ored driftings of the flood.
XV.
For them the Ceylon diver held his breath,
And went all naked to the hungry shark;
For them his ears gush'd blood; for them in death
The seal on the cold ice with piteous bark
Lay full of darts; for them alone did seethe
A thousand men in troubles wide and dark:

Half-ignorant, they turn'd an easy wheel,
That set sharp racks at work, to pinch and peel.
XVI.
Why were they proud? Because their marble founts
Gush'd with more pride than do a wretch's tears?--
Why were they proud? Because fair orange-mounts
Were of more soft ascent than lazar stairs?--
Why were they proud? Because red-lin'd accounts
Were richer than the songs of Grecian years?--
Why were they proud? again we ask aloud,
Why in the name of Glory were they proud?
XVII.
Yet were these Florentines as self-retired
In hungry pride and gainful cowardice,
As two close Hebrews in that land inspired,
Paled in and vineyarded from beggar-spies,
The hawks of ship-mast forests--the untired
And pannier'd mules for ducats and old lies--
Quick cat's-paws on the generous stray-away,--
Great wits in Spanish, Tuscan, and Malay.
XVIII.
How was it these same ledger-men could spy
Fair Isabella in her downy nest?
How could they find out in Lorenzo's eye
A straying from his toil? Hot Egypt's pest
Into their vision covetous and sly!
How could these money-bags see east and west?--
Yet so they did--and every dealer fair
Must see behind, as doth the hunted hare.
XIX.
O eloquent and famed Boccaccio!
Of thee we now should ask forgiving boon,
And of thy spicy myrtles as they blow,
And of thy roses amorous of the moon,
And of thy lilies, that do paler grow
Now they can no more hear thy ghittern's tune,
For venturing syllables that ill beseem

The quiet glooms of such a piteous theme.

XX.

Grant thou a pardon here, and then the tale
Shall move on soberly, as it is meet;
There is no other crime, no mad assail
To make old prose in modern rhyme more sweet:
But it is done--succeed the verse or fail--
To honour thee, and thy gone spirit greet;
To stead thee as a verse in English tongue,
An echo of thee in the north-wind sung.

XXI.

These brethren having found by many signs
What love Lorenzo for their sister had,
And how she lov'd him too, each unconfines
His bitter thoughts to other, well nigh mad
That he, the servant of their trade designs,
Should in their sister's love be blithe and glad,
When 'twas their plan to coax her by degrees
To some high noble and his olive-trees.

XXII.

And many a jealous conference had they,
And many times they bit their lips alone,
Before they fix'd upon a surest way
To make the youngster for his crime atone;
And at the last, these men of cruel clay
Cut Mercy with a sharp knife to the bone;
For they resolved in some forest dim
To kill Lorenzo, and there bury him.

XXIII.

So on a pleasant morning, as he leant
Into the sun-rise, o'er the balustrade
Of the garden-terrace, towards him they bent
Their footing through the dews; and to him said,
"You seem there in the quiet of content,
"Lorenzo, and we are most loth to invade
"Calm speculation; but if you are wise,
"Bestride your steed while cold is in the skies.

XXIV.

"To-day we purpose, ay, this hour we mount
"To spur three leagues towards the Apennine;
"Come down, we pray thee, ere the hot sun count
"His dewy rosary on the eglantine."
Lorenzo, courteously as he was wont,
Bow'd a fair greeting to these serpents' whine;
And went in haste, to get in readiness,
With belt, and spur, and bracing huntsman's dress.

XXV.

And as he to the court-yard pass'd along,
Each third step did he pause, and listen'd oft
If he could hear his lady's matin-song,
Or the light whisper of her footstep soft;
And as he thus over his passion hung,
He heard a laugh full musical aloft;
When, looking up, he saw her features bright
Smile through an in-door lattice, all delight.

XXVI.

"Love, Isabel!" said he, "I was in pain
"Lest I should miss to bid thee a good morrow:
"Ah! what if I should lose thee, when so fain
"I am to stifle all the heavy sorrow
"Of a poor three hours' absence? but we'll gain
"Out of the amorous dark what day doth borrow.
"Good bye! I'll soon be back."--"Good bye!" said she:--
And as he went she chanted merrily.

XXVII.

So the two brothers and their murder'd man
Rode past fair Florence, to where Arno's stream
Gurgles through straiten'd banks, and still doth fan
Itself with dancing bulrush, and the bream
Keeps head against the freshets. Sick and wan
The brothers' faces in the ford did seem,
Lorenzo's flush with love.--They pass'd the water
Into a forest quiet for the slaughter.

XXVIII.

There was Lorenzo slain and buried in,
There in that forest did his great love cease;
Ah! when a soul doth thus its freedom win,
It aches in loneliness--is ill at peace
As the break-covert blood-hounds of such sin:
They dipp'd their swords in the water, and did tease
Their horses homeward, with convulsed spur,
Each richer by his being a murderer.
XXIX.
They told their sister how, with sudden speed,
Lorenzo had ta'en ship for foreign lands,
Because of some great urgency and need
In their affairs, requiring trusty hands.
Poor Girl! put on thy stifling widow's weed,
And 'scape at once from Hope's accursed bands;
To-day thou wilt not see him, nor to-morrow,
And the next day will be a day of sorrow.
XXX.
She weeps alone for pleasures not to be;
Sorely she wept until the night came on,
And then, instead of love, O misery!
She brooded o'er the luxury alone:
His image in the dusk she seem'd to see,
And to the silence made a gentle moan,
Spreading her perfect arms upon the air,
And on her couch low murmuring, "Where? O where?"
XXXI.
But Selfishness, Love's cousin, held not long
Its fiery vigil in her single breast;
She fretted for the golden hour, and hung
Upon the time with feverish unrest--
Not long--for soon into her heart a throng
Of higher occupants, a richer zest,
Came tragic; passion not to be subdued,
And sorrow for her love in travels rude.
XXXII.
In the mid days of autumn, on their eves

The breath of Winter comes from far away,
And the sick west continually bereaves
Of some gold tinge, and plays a roundelay
Of death among the bushes and the leaves,
To make all bare before he dares to stray
From his north cavern. So sweet Isabel
By gradual decay from beauty fell,

XXXIII.

Because Lorenzo came not. Oftentimes
She ask'd her brothers, with an eye all pale,
Striving to be itself, what dungeon climes
Could keep him off so long? They spake a tale
Time after time, to quiet her. Their crimes
Came on them, like a smoke from Hinnom's vale;
And every night in dreams they groan'd aloud,
To see their sister in her snowy shroud.

XXXIV.

And she had died in drowsy ignorance,
But for a thing more deadly dark than all;
It came like a fierce potion, drunk by chance,
Which saves a sick man from the feather'd pall
For some few gasping moments; like a lance,
Waking an Indian from his cloudy hall
With cruel pierce, and bringing him again
Sense of the gnawing fire at heart and brain.

XXXV.

It was a vision.--In the drowsy gloom,
The dull of midnight, at her couch's foot
Lorenzo stood, and wept: the forest tomb
Had marr'd his glossy hair which once could shoot
Lustre into the sun, and put cold doom
Upon his lips, and taken the soft lute
From his lorn voice, and past his loamed ears
Had made a miry channel for his tears.

XXXVI.

Strange sound it was, when the pale shadow spake;
For there was striving, in its piteous tongue,

To speak as when on earth it was awake,
And Isabella on its music hung:
Languor there was in it, and tremulous shake,
As in a palsied Druid's harp unstrung;
And through it moan'd a ghostly under-song,
Like hoarse night-gusts sepulchral briars among.
XXXVII.
Its eyes, though wild, were still all dewy bright
With love, and kept all phantom fear aloof
From the poor girl by magic of their light,
The while it did unthread the horrid woof
Of the late darken'd time,--the murderous spite
Of pride and avarice,--the dark pine roof
In the forest,--and the sodden turfed dell,
Where, without any word, from stabs he fell.
XXXVIII.
Saying moreover, "Isabel, my sweet!
"Red whortle-berries droop above my head,
"And a large flint-stone weighs upon my feet;
"Around me beeches and high chestnuts shed
"Their leaves and prickly nuts; a sheep-fold bleat
"Comes from beyond the river to my bed:
"Go, shed one tear upon my heather-bloom,
"And it shall comfort me within the tomb.
XXXIX.
"I am a shadow now, alas! alas!
"Upon the skirts of human-nature dwelling
"Alone: I chant alone the holy mass,
"While little sounds of life are round me knelling,
"And glossy bees at noon do fieldward pass,
"And many a chapel bell the hour is telling,
"Paining me through: those sounds grow strange to me,
"And thou art distant in Humanity.
XL.
"I know what was, I feel full well what is,
"And I should rage, if spirits could go mad;
"Though I forget the taste of earthly bliss,

"That paleness warms my grave, as though I had
"A Seraph chosen from the bright abyss
"To be my spouse: thy paleness makes me glad;
"Thy beauty grows upon me, and I feel
"A greater love through all my essence steal."
XLI.
The Spirit mourn'd "Adieu!"--dissolv'd, and left
The atom darkness in a slow turmoil;
As when of healthful midnight sleep bereft,
Thinking on rugged hours and fruitless toil,
We put our eyes into a pillowy cleft,
And see the spangly gloom froth up and boil:
It made sad Isabella's eyelids ache,
And in the dawn she started up awake;
XLII.
"Ha! ha!" said she, "I knew not this hard life,
"I thought the worst was simple misery;
"I thought some Fate with pleasure or with strife
"Portion'd us--happy days, or else to die;
"But there is crime--a brother's bloody knife!
"Sweet Spirit, thou hast school'd my infancy:
"I'll visit thee for this, and kiss thine eyes,
"And greet thee morn and even in the skies."
XLIII.
When the full morning came, she had devised
How she might secret to the forest hie;
How she might find the clay, so dearly prized,
And sing to it one latest lullaby;
How her short absence might be unsurmised,
While she the inmost of the dream would try.
Resolv'd, she took with her an aged nurse,
And went into that dismal forest-hearse.
XLIV.
See, as they creep along the river side,
How she doth whisper to that aged Dame,
And, after looking round the champaign wide,
Shows her a knife.--"What feverous hectic flame

"Burns in thee, child?--What good can thee betide,
"That thou should'st smile again?"--The evening came,
And they had found Lorenzo's earthy bed;
The flint was there, the berries at his head.
XLV.
Who hath not loiter'd in a green church-yard,
And let his spirit, like a demon-mole,
Work through the clayey soil and gravel hard,
To see skull, coffin'd bones, and funeral stole;
Pitying each form that hungry Death hath marr'd,
And filling it once more with human soul?
Ah! this is holiday to what was felt
When Isabella by Lorenzo knelt.
XLVI.
She gaz'd into the fresh-thrown mould, as though
One glance did fully all its secrets tell;
Clearly she saw, as other eyes would know
Pale limbs at bottom of a crystal well;
Upon the murderous spot she seem'd to grow,
Like to a native lily of the dell:
Then with her knife, all sudden, she began
To dig more fervently than misers can.
XLVII.
Soon she turn'd up a soiled glove, whereon
Her silk had play'd in purple phantasies,
She kiss'd it with a lip more chill than stone,
And put it in her bosom, where it dries
And freezes utterly unto the bone
Those dainties made to still an infant's cries:
Then 'gan she work again; nor stay'd her care,
But to throw back at times her veiling hair.
XLVIII.
That old nurse stood beside her wondering,
Until her heart felt pity to the core
At sight of such a dismal labouring,
And so she kneeled, with her locks all hoar,
And put her lean hands to the horrid thing:

Three hours they labour'd at this travail sore;
At last they felt the kernel of the grave,
And Isabella did not stamp and rave.
XLIX.
Ah! wherefore all this wormy circumstance?
Why linger at the yawning tomb so long?
O for the gentleness of old Romance,
The simple plaining of a minstrel's song!
Fair reader, at the old tale take a glance,
For here, in truth, it doth not well belong
To speak:--O turn thee to the very tale,
And taste the music of that vision pale.
L.
With duller steel than the Persèan sword
They cut away no formless monster's head,
But one, whose gentleness did well accord
With death, as life. The ancient harps have said,
Love never dies, but lives, immortal Lord:
If Love impersonate was ever dead,
Pale Isabella kiss'd it, and low moan'd.
'Twas love; cold,--dead indeed, but not dethroned.
LI.
In anxious secrecy they took it home,
And then the prize was all for Isabel:
She calm'd its wild hair with a golden comb,
And all around each eye's sepulchral cell
Pointed each fringed lash; the smeared loam
With tears, as chilly as a dripping well,
She drench'd away:--and still she comb'd, and kept
Sighing all day--and still she kiss'd, and wept.
LII.
Then in a silken scarf,--sweet with the dews
Of precious flowers pluck'd in Araby,
And divine liquids come with odorous ooze
Through the cold serpent pipe refreshfully,--
She wrapp'd it up; and for its tomb did choose
A garden-pot, wherein she laid it by,

And cover'd it with mould, and o'er it set
Sweet Basil, which her tears kept ever wet.
LIII.
And she forgot the stars, the moon, and sun,
And she forgot the blue above the trees,
And she forgot the dells where waters run,
And she forgot the chilly autumn breeze;
She had no knowledge when the day was done,
And the new morn she saw not: but in peace
Hung over her sweet Basil evermore,
And moisten'd it with tears unto the core.
LIV.
And so she ever fed it with thin tears,
Whence thick, and green, and beautiful it grew,
So that it smelt more balmy than its peers
Of Basil-tufts in Florence; for it drew
Nurture besides, and life, from human fears,
From the fast mouldering head there shut from view:
So that the jewel, safely casketed,
Came forth, and in perfumed leafits spread.
LV.
O Melancholy, linger here awhile!
O Music, Music, breathe despondingly!
O Echo, Echo, from some sombre isle,
Unknown, Lethean, sigh to us--O sigh!
Spirits in grief, lift up your heads, and smile;
Lift up your heads, sweet Spirits, heavily,
And make a pale light in your cypress glooms,
Tinting with silver wan your marble tombs.
LVI.
Moan hither, all ye syllables of woe,
From the deep throat of sad Melpomene!
Through bronzed lyre in tragic order go,
And touch the strings into a mystery;
Sound mournfully upon the winds and low;
For simple Isabel is soon to be
Among the dead: She withers, like a palm

Cut by an Indian for its juicy balm.

LVII.

O leave the palm to wither by itself;
Let not quick Winter chill its dying hour!--
It may not be--those Baalites of pelf,
Her brethren, noted the continual shower
From her dead eyes; and many a curious elf,
Among her kindred, wonder'd that such dower
Of youth and beauty should be thrown aside
By one mark'd out to be a Noble's bride.

LVIII.

And, furthermore, her brethren wonder'd much
Why she sat drooping by the Basil green,
And why it flourish'd, as by magic touch;
Greatly they wonder'd what the thing might mean:
They could not surely give belief, that such
A very nothing would have power to wean
Her from her own fair youth, and pleasures gay,
And even remembrance of her love's delay.

LIX.

Therefore they watch'd a time when they might sift
This hidden whim; and long they watch'd in vain;
For seldom did she go to chapel-shrift,
And seldom felt she any hunger-pain;
And when she left, she hurried back, as swift
As bird on wing to breast its eggs again;
And, patient as a hen-bird, sat her there
Beside her Basil, weeping through her hair.

LX.

Yet they contriv'd to steal the Basil-pot,
And to examine it in secret place:
The thing was vile with green and livid spot,
And yet they knew it was Lorenzo's face:
The guerdon of their murder they had got,
And so left Florence in a moment's space,
Never to turn again.--Away they went,
With blood upon their heads, to banishment.

LXI.

O Melancholy, turn thine eyes away!
O Music, Music, breathe despondingly!
O Echo, Echo, on some other day,
From isles Lethean, sigh to us--O sigh!
Spirits of grief, sing not your "Well-a-way!"
For Isabel, sweet Isabel, will die;
Will die a death too lone and incomplete,
Now they have ta'en away her Basil sweet.

LXII.

Piteous she look'd on dead and senseless things,
Asking for her lost Basil amorously:
And with melodious chuckle in the strings
Of her lorn voice, she oftentimes would cry
After the Pilgrim in his wanderings,
To ask him where her Basil was; and why
'Twas hid from her: "For cruel 'tis," said she,
"To steal my Basil-pot away from me."

LXIII.

And so she pined, and so she died forlorn,
Imploring for her Basil to the last.
No heart was there in Florence but did mourn
In pity of her love, so overcast.
And a sad ditty of this story born
From mouth to mouth through all the country pass'd:
Still is the burthen sung--"O cruelty,
"To steal my Basil-pot away from me!"

ABOUT THE AUTHOR

John Keats was an English poet, born in London in 1795 or 1796, died in Rome, Feb. 27, 1821. He was sent at an early age with his two brothers to a school in Enfield, where he remained until his 15th year. He seems to have been careless of the ordinary school distinctions, but read whatever authors attracted his fancy. He never advanced in his classical studies beyond Latin, and his knowledge of Greek mythology was derived from Lempriere's dictionary and Tooke's "Pantheon;" a singular fact considering the thoroughly Hellenic spirit which imbues some of his works. In 1810 he was removed from school, and apprenticed for five years to a surgeon in Edmonton.

His earliest known verses are the lines "In Imitation of Spenser." About the same time he became acquainted with Homer through Chapman's translation, and commemorated his emotions in the sonnet, "On first looking into Chapman's Homer." Upon the completion of his apprenticeship he removed to London to "walk the hospitals," and made the acquaintance of Leigh Hunt, Haydon, Hazlitt, Godwin, and other literary men, incited by whose praise he published a volume of poems, comprising sonnets, poetical epistles, and other small pieces, which excited little attention. He soon perceived that the profession of a surgeon was unfitted for him, both on account of his extreme nervousness in the performance of operations, and of the state of his health; and in the spring of 1817 he was induced by symptoms of consumption to make a visit to the country. During this absence he commenced his "Endymion," which, with some miscellaneous pieces, was published in the following year.

Keats had allied himself with a political and literary coterie obnoxious to the "Quarterly Review" and "Blackwood's Magazine," and the appearance of a volume of poems by a new writer of the "cockney school" was the signal for an attack upon him by these periodicals, the bitterness of which savored more of personal animosity than of critical discernment. The insulting allusions to his private affairs and his family aroused in the poet no other feeling than contempt or indignation; and if we may judge from his letters, far from being crushed in spirit by the virulence of his reviewers, he would have been much more inclined to inflict personal chastisement upon them if he had met them. Byron in "Don Juan," and Shelley in "Adonais," have apparently confirmed the notion that his sensitive nature on this occasion received a shock from which it never recovered; but the effect of the criticism has been greatly exaggerated.

His health was failing rapidly, but from other causes. His younger brother's death in the autumn of 1818 affected him deeply, and about the same time he experienced a passion for a lady of remarkable beauty, the effect of which upon a frame worn by disease was fatal. His little patrimony became exhausted, and he began to think of making literature his profession. While preparing a third volume for the press he was attacked with a violent spitting of blood. After a long illness he recovered sufficiently to think of resuming his literary avocations, but found his mind too unstrung by sickness and the passion which had such an influence over him. In this emergency he had nearly determined to accept the berth of surgeon in an Indiaman, when a return of the previous alarming symptoms made it apparent that nothing but a winter in a milder climate would offer a chance of saving his life.

Before his departure he published a volume containing his odes on the "Nightingale" and the "Grecian Urn," the poems of "Lamia," "The Eve of St. Agnes," "Isabella," &c., and the magnificent fragment of "Hyperion." In September, 1820, Keats left England with Mr. Severn, a young artist and a devoted friend, who never left his bedside. He lingered a few months at Naples and Rome, and died at the latter place after much suffering. A few days before his death he said that he "felt the daisies growing over him." He was buried in the Protestant cemetery in Rome, near the spot where Shelley's ashes were afterward interred; and upon his tomb was inscribed the epitaph, dictated by himself: "Here lies one whose name was writ in water." His modest hope that "after his death he would be among the poets of England," has been more fully realized than he could have anticipated; and his influence can be traced in the poetic development of many later writers.

THE POET KEATS

His was the soul, once pent in English clay,
Whereby ungrateful England seemed to hold
The sweet Narcissus, parted from his stream,--
Endymion, not unmindful of his dream,
Like a weak bird the flock has left behind.

Untimely notes the poet sung alone,
Checked by the chilling frosts of words unkind;
And his grieved soul, some thousand years astray,
Paled like the moon in most unwelcome day.

His speech betrayed him ere his heart grew cold;
With morning freshness to the world he told
Of man's first love, and fearless creed of youth,
When Beauty he believed the type of Truth.

In the vexed glories of unquiet Troy,
So might to Helen's jealous ear discourse
The flute, first tuned on Ida's haunted hill,
Against OEnone's coming, to betray
In what sweet solitude her shepherd lay.

Yet, Poet-Priest! the world shall ever thrill
To thy loved theme, its charm undying still!
Hearts in their youth are Greek as Homer's song,
And all Olympus half contents the boy,
Who from the quarries of abounding joy
Brings his white idols without thought of wrong.

With reverent hand he sets each votive stone,
And last, the altar "To the God Unknown."

As in our dreams the face that we love best
Blooms as at first, while we ourselves grow old,--
As the returning Spring in sunlight throws
Through prison-bars, on graves, its ardent gold,--
And as the splendors of a Syrian rose
Lie unreproved upon the saddest breast,--
So mythic story fits a changing world:
Still the bark drifts with sails forever furled.
An unschooled Fancy deemed the work her own,
While mystic meaning through each fable shone.

(featured in The Atlantic Monthly, 1858)

www.ingramcontent.com/pod-product-compliance
Lightning Source LLC
Chambersburg PA
CBHW071323130626
46556CB00004B/1713